"What took you so long?"

"Ah, you missed me," Matt said. "That's a promising sign. We men, being such virile creatures, have to shave."

"It can't take forty-five minutes," Cathy retorted.

"I do my best thinking under the shower."

"That's very handy, isn't it? In an emergency, I mean, to have to scoot around till you find a shower."

"Luckily, one was handy in this emergency. I had a lot of thinking to do." His bemused smile suggested that he'd been thinking about her.

"What's the matter, did you miss one whisker?" she asked.

He ran his palm over his cheek. She could almost feel his taut skin, smooth from the razor.

"Come and feel for yourself," he said, tempting her.

"I'll take your word for it."

"I didn't offer you my word. I suggested you feel for yourself."

She didn't trust the way he was staring at her, with that dreamy, sexy look in his eyes. She didn't trust herself to get close to him, either.

"I don't see any stubble." She picked up her purse and headed for the door, with Matt following behind her.

"Coward."

Dear Reader,

May... the month when flowers—and love—are in full bloom—especially here at Silhouette Romance. And as you know, spring is also that special time of year when a man's thoughts turn to love. Be they the boy next door or a handsome, mysterious stranger, our heroes are no exception! Six lucky heroines are about to find their dreams of happy-ever-after come true as once again, Silhouette Romance sweeps you away with heartwarming, poignant stories of love.

In the months to come, we'll be publishing romances by many of your all-time favorites, including Diana Palmer, Brittany Young and Annette Broadrick. And coming next month, Nora Roberts will launch her not-to-be-missed Calhoun Women Series with the June Silhouette Romance, *Courting Catherine*.

WRITTEN IN THE STARS is a very special event for 1991. Each month, we're proud to present a Silhouette Romance that focuses on the hero—and his astrological sign. May features the stubborn-but-loveable Taurus man. Our authors and editors have created this delightfully romantic series especially for you, the reader, and we'd love to hear what you think. After all, at Silhouette Romance, we take our readers' comments to heart!

Please write to us at Silhouette Romance
300 East 42nd Street
New York, New York
10017

We look forward to hearing from you!

Sincerely,

Valerie Susan Hayward
Senior Editor

JOAN SMITH

Her Lucky
Break

Silhouette *Romance*

Published by Silhouette Books New York

America's Publisher of Contemporary Romance

SILHOUETTE BOOKS
300 E. 42nd St., New York, N.Y. 10017

HER LUCKY BREAK

ISBN: 0-373-08795-0

First Silhouette Books printing May 1991

Printed in the U.S.A.

Books by Joan Smith

Silhouette Romance

Next Year's Blonde #234
Caprice #255
From Now On #269
Chance of a Lifetime #288
Best of Enemies #302
Trouble in Paradise #315
Future Perfect #325
Tender Takeover #343
The Yielding Art #354
The Infamous Madam X #430
Where There's a Will #452
Dear Corrie #546
If You Love Me #562
By Hook or By Crook #591
After the Storm #617
Maybe Next Time #635
It Takes Two #656
Thrill of the Chase #669
Sealed with a Kiss #711
Her Nest Egg #755
Her Lucky Break #795

JOAN SMITH

has written many Regency romances, but likes working with the greater freedom of contemporaries. She also enjoys mysteries and Gothics, collects Japanese porcelain and is a passionate gardener. A native of Canada, she is the mother of three.

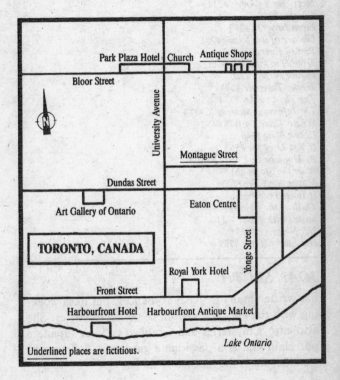

Park Plaza Hotel | Church | Antique Shops

Bloor Street

University Avenue

N

Montague Street

Dundas Street

Art Gallery of Ontario

Eaton Centre

Yonge Street

TORONTO, CANADA

Royal York Hotel

Front Street

Harbourfront Hotel | Harbourfront Antique Market

Lake Ontario

Underlined places are fictitious.

Chapter One

Cathy Auden had already taken two pictures of the quaint stone church where her parents had been married a quarter of a century before. By coincidence, there was another wedding in progress that day. Her parents would hardly recognize the church now, with the high-rise apartment soaring behind it. An incongruous place for a modern apartment building, practically attached to a Gothic church. Of course, this Yorkville area of Toronto had become very chic during the twenty-odd years since her parents had lived here, and the economics of real estate took precedence over aesthetics in large cities.

She glanced at her watch, trying to decide whether to go back to the hotel or wait to see the bride's exit from the church. It was a lovely day for a wedding, early in June, with the sun spilling golden beams from the azure sky. Suddenly the door opened, and the organ strains of the wedding recessional swelled out from the church. The couple would appear any minute now, so Cathy decided to wait.

The size of the crowd suggested it was a celebrity wedding. The stretch limos were lined up for a block, with reporters and cameramen everywhere, jostling elbows and joking. Even a crew of teenagers had turned out for the event, and on a school day, too. Cathy decided it must be a show biz affair. She'd wait and snap a picture of the bride and groom, since this picture was to be a memento of her parents' wedding. They would have been married twenty-five years next week. A quarter of a century! It seemed an eternity to Cathy, who had only been on the earth for twenty-two years herself.

"They're coming!" one of the teenagers yelled. Cathy vied with the other photographers for a good shot. A swell of excitement rose in the throng, then turned to silence as all eyes strained for a view of the bride. Cathy gasped, not quite able to hold back a little gurgle of laughter. The bride had shocking pink hair and wore what appeared to be white short shorts. A second look told her it was a white mini-wedding-dress, topped with a long veil of violet lace. The groom was resplendent in a gold lamé tuxedo. She recognized him as Wolfe, a reigning rock star. Lion seemed a more appropriate name, with his mane of unruly hair. Well, that explained the swarm of adoring adolescents.

Cathy was disappointed that the couple looked so unconventional. Then, with a chuckle she lined her camera up for a shot. This would really highlight the changes that twenty-five years had wrought. Her mom and dad would get a laugh out of the outfits. As she lined up her shot again, a dalmatian escaped its owner and bounded closer for a look at the bride and groom. He sat on his haunches, cocked his head to one side and gave a questioning look.

Cathy clicked the picture and quickly advanced the film for another shot. More people than her parents would like to have a copy of this picture. Her brother, Rob, was a big Wolfe fan. Someone rushed forward to remove the dog.

Cathy waited, and when the bridesmaid and best man joined the bride and groom, she snapped again. She wasn't a Wolfe fan herself, but she was pretty sure Wolfe's best man was also his lead guitarist. Rob would die for this!

A third long-haired man was called in to pose, and Cathy lined up another shot. Just as the shutter opened, a shadow passed swiftly in front of her. Someone had blocked the bridal couple, spoiling the shot. She gave a *tsk* of annoyance and looked up to see who had ruined the picture.

A very average-looking man in a tweed jacket and matching cap was hurrying past. The only reason she noticed the jacket was that her father had one just like it. The man stopped and looked over his shoulder, startled. When he realized she was frowning, he raised his cap and said "Sorry, did I spoil your picture?"

"That's all right. I'll get another," she said.

The man scurried away with a last peek over his shoulder. A pair of dark glasses hid most of his face, but his hair was a strange henna shade that looked unnatural.

Cathy returned to her task without giving the man another thought. She didn't notice that he stopped at the corner, turned back and stared at her with a worried frown. She didn't see him loitering amid the crowd, waiting to see where she went. She was snapping the last shot on her film, a picture of Wolfe kissing his bride, when the man took to his heels. He managed to catch a cab at the corner of the street and was whisked away, while a tall, angry young man looked in vain for a cab to follow him.

When Cathy had taken her last shot, she slung her camera over her shoulder and walked along to her hotel, enjoying the warm sun on her shoulders, the jostling city crowd and the expensive boutiques that lined Bloor Street. She smiled at the memory of the pictures she had just taken. She'd get the one of Wolfe and his bride and the dalmatian blown up for Rob. Maybe get it made into a poster. A glance at her watch showed her it was ten to twelve. Incipient hunger pangs reminded her she had had only a brioche and coffee for breakfast.

Cathy turned in at the elegant Park Plaza Hotel, strode briskly through the marble lobby, stopping only at the washroom to tidy up before entering the coffee shop. After she had run a brush through her chin-length dark hair and washed her hands, she removed the film from her camera and put in a new roll. This done, she proceeded to the coffee shop. It was crowded at lunch hour. She felt lucky to get the last empty table, a table for two. As it was warm in the crowded room, she removed her red jacket, placing it over her camera and purse on the extra chair.

She ordered a Spanish omelet, wincing at the price, but the place was beautiful. This was her first holiday without her family, paid for by herself, and she had decided to go in style. The tour she had started out with had left Toronto the night before, but she was to stay on a few days alone. Tuesday and Wednesday had been filled with tours of the city and shows at night. It had all been exciting and glamorous. The last days were to be more personal, a sort of return to her roots.

Cathy had been born and spent the first three years of her life here, but of course the few vague memories she retained centered on her parents and home. It was odd her parents had never been back to Toronto, since they only lived a few hundred miles away, in Schenectady. But Mom's widowed mother had died, and Dad was from Schenectady, so they moved there and had never come back.

It was strange, too, that her father's decision to take a holiday in Toronto twenty-five years ago had led to his marrying a Canadian. He would never have met Mom if it weren't for that holiday. And the accident, of course. Dad had broken his leg when he slipped off a curb, and Mom was his nurse at the hospital. "My lucky break," he called it.

"Love at first sight," they both said. Their love was still going strong a quarter of a century later. The romantic story of their chance meeting was one that her parents had often repeated. Now Cathy was on holiday in Toronto—maybe she'd get lucky. Her lips curved in a soft smile as she thought of her parents.

Cathy meant to make a few pilgrimages: to the house her parents had lived in in Etobicoke, the church where they had been married, the hospital where she herself had been born. She meant to take pictures of all those places and put them into an album for her parents' twenty-fifth anniversary. She knew the real-estate office her father used to work in had been taken over by a chain. The building had been torn down, so there was nothing to see there. Dad hadn't cared much for selling houses, anyway. He wanted to be a policeman, like his father before him. Now he was a lieutenant detective, and Cathy was following in his footsteps. She was still on the bottom rung, but she meant to be a career cop, like her dad.

It often seemed to Cathy that her parents had led a charmed life. They had met, fallen in love, gotten married, had the family they wanted—a boy and a girl—and Dad had the job he wanted. Mom had interrupted her career to raise the children, and later stepped back into her profession of nursing with no real problems along the way. Everything seemed more complicated now.

Wrapped up in her private thoughts, she didn't notice that the waiter was casting curious glances at her. He came forward and said politely, "I wonder if you would mind sharing your table, ma'am? As you can see, we're crowded, and there is an empty seat here."

She cast a guilty look from the empty chair to the growing throng at the door. "Not at all," she said, looking to see who would be joining her. The waiter led a man forward. As she glanced around the room, she noticed she wasn't the

only single person at a table that would hold more than one.
The others weren't having anyone placed at their table. Why
had the waiter picked on her? She wasn't vain, but she had
been hit on before, and it occurred to her that the man might
have bribed the waiter to arrange this meeting.

The man who was joining her smiled and nodded. "It's
very kind of you to share your table," he said in a friendly
voice. Any rising annoyance Cathy felt quickly subsided at
that smile. He was terribly handsome! A pair of pearly gray
eyes sparkled dramatically in his weathered face. His ebony
black hair, straight as a dye, was worn in a short, business
cut that lent dignity to his appearance. As he drew out his
chair, one wayward lock tumbled forward. She liked that,
too; it made him seem less formidable.

Cathy let her glance linger a moment, observing his
straight, shapely nose and strongly cut jaw. If it weren't for
that one shock of hair out of place and his smile, he'd look
downright severe. He wore a sky blue oxford shirt, a dark
suit of English tailoring and a silk tie the shade of raspber-
ries. His shoulders, broad and straight like a soldier's, lent
him an air of authority. He looked like a man who knew
where he was going and what he was doing. She had a vague
sense that he was used to getting his own way.

"They're crowded at noon hour. It seems selfish to waste
the seat," she replied coolly. She didn't want to give him the
idea she was an easy pickup.

She noticed then that he was carrying a camera, too.
When he began looking for someplace to put it, she realized her possessions filled the spare chair. "I'll take those,"
she said, and began to rise.

"Allow me." He lifted her red jacket, looking around for
some place to hang it.

"You can put it on the back of my chair. I'd better keep
my purse, too," she said, reaching for it. "I can hang my

camera and purse under my coat." There was a moment of fumbling confusion while he helped her arrange her items.

The man's downcast eyes hid the gleam of interest in the camera. Had she managed to snap Carr's picture? Was that why Carr had been speaking to her? If this woman had captured Carr's ugly face on film, he must be in a fever to get it back. Ironic that she had succeeded without even trying, whereas he had been trying in vain for months. On the other hand, she might be a friend or colleague of Carr's. What was Carr doing in Canada, anyway?

"My name's Matt Wilson," he said, and reached across the white linen cloth to shake her hand in a firm grip.

She felt the strength in his elegantly long fingers, and noticed the simple gold signet ring on his right hand. His left hand rested on the table. No ring. Not married, or just not wearing a ring?

"Cathy Auden," she replied briefly before returning her attention to her omelet.

The name didn't ring any bells for Matt, but then she could be using an alias if she was mixed up in Carr's business. "Are you a tourist, Cathy, or a Torontonian?" he asked, picking up the menu.

"A tourist. Just visiting."

"That's an American accent, I think?"

"Yes, I'm from Schenectady."

The waiter came, and Matt ordered a New York strip steak, medium rare. As soon as the waiter left, Matt asked, "Do you mind if we talk, or would you rather eat in private? I don't want to compound the offense of barging in on you by pestering you with chatter if you'd rather not."

As he seemed to be polite and not on the make, Cathy decided to be friendly. "Feel free to talk. It's nice to have company."

"Did you come to Toronto alone?" he asked. Now that he was safely ensconced, he had a moment to study her. This

Cathy Auden was attractive. He liked those bright-eyed, intelligent-looking women. Her hair, which he had thought was black, glinted with auburn highlights under the lamps. A flash of brilliant green eyes, heavily fringed with long lashes, examined him frankly. He read the interest in them, and warmed to it. Her complexion was of the peaches-and-cream variety, with a beguiling display of freckles across the bridge of her nose. He already knew from having followed her into the hotel that she had a trim derriere and admirable ankles. The creamy silk shirt she wore lent her an air of innocence. He noticed the slender gold chain at her neck, with a tiny gold wishbone pendant. Was she superstitious? She looked far too rational for that.

"I came with a tour group, but they've left now. I'm remaining a few days on my own," she said nonchalantly, as if she did this sort of thing all the time. "Are you from Toronto, Mr. Wilson?"

"Matt, please. No, I'm here on a holiday, too," he lied blandly. It sounded a trifle suspicious, her staying on here alone. If, on the other hand, she was innocent, people didn't like to "get involved" in criminal matters. "What do you do when you're not on holiday?" he asked.

"I'm a cop," she said proudly.

Matt blinked in astonishment. Of course, he knew there were such things as lady cops, but he had always assumed they'd be bigger, older, less feminine looking. At a guess he would have taken Cathy for a white-collar worker of some kind. Tops on the list of things he *didn't* need was a cop, lady or otherwise. In his work he had to skirt a few rules. Nothing major, of course, but as sure as he made an illegal entry, all in the way of catching a criminal, the law would be there to arrest the innocent, while the real criminal got away.

Looking at her again, he noticed that severely-tailored jacket, almost like a uniform. If he enlisted her help, the first thing she'd want to do would be to call in the local police, who would ask what the formal charges against Carr were. How did you lay charges against a man who was supposed to be dead? And if he convinced her he wasn't crazy, it wouldn't be long before she took over and scared Carr off. That was the police's idea of help. Well, they had their rules, of course, but he had his own way of working.

"Isn't that dangerous work for a woman?" he asked.

She gave a deprecating grin. "Not that dangerous in Schenectady. As a rookie I spend a lot of time visiting schools to give safety lectures, that sort of thing. I'm really looking forward to making detective."

Matt smiled noncommittally. Carr wasn't actively wanted by the police. His crime was against the insurance company that Matt represented. A one-million-dollar job.

"Is this your first visit to Toronto?" he asked.

"I was born here. I haven't been back since I was a kid."

Matt asked how she had come to leave, and she found herself explaining that her parents had met and married here, but her dad was actually an American. From Matt's leading questions, she assumed he was interested. He felt he was listening to a fairy tale. Did anyone really have such a storybook upbringing as the one she described? It certainly bore no resemblance to his own chaotic youth.

Of course, Cathy didn't go into all the romantic details of her parents' meeting to a perfect stranger. She just sketched briefly where and how they had met and the sort of life they lived. "Where are you from, Matt?" she asked when she realized she had been more or less monopolizing the conversation.

"Chicago. I'm a stockbroker," he replied, and felt a twinge of guilt at deceiving her. It might be fun to tell her the truth and ask her help, but really a rookie from Schenectady wouldn't be much help. This one, with her frank smile and wide green eyes, would be too much of a distraction.

No clever reply occurred to Cathy. Her familiarity with stockbrokers was limited to TV and the newspapers, where they weren't enjoying a particularly good reputation at that time. She had an impression that stockbrokers made a great deal of money without working very hard for it. "Oh," she said, her voice tinged with doubt.

He lifted his eyes and grinned at her. "We're not all crooks," he said as if he'd been reading her mind. That boyish grin removed any lingering idea that he was trying to hit on her. It was friendly, open and quite devastatingly attractive. She liked the way the skin crinkled at the corners of his eyes. Her heart seemed to swell and fill her chest when he smiled. "Inside traders are the lepers in our field. They smear us all—like the few bad cops you read about, guys on the take." A challenging look told her he was retaliating.

"I'd never accept a bribe!" she objected. "My family have been policemen for two generations. We're totally honest."

"So is Stack Bedford, the brokerage house I represent." Matt realized he was enjoying himself, and felt guilty for the lapse. He had bribed his way to this table to do some brain picking, and it was time he got down to it. To steer the conversation around to the camera, he asked, "Are you taking some pictures to show your folks? I see you have your camera along."

"Yes, you too," she mentioned, glancing at his camera. "I want to show Mom and Dad how Toronto's changed. I got a shot of Wolfe's wedding. Wolfe, the rock star."

"Really?" he asked, feigning surprise. "I caught a look at it myself in passing. An interesting affair. Did you get some good shots?"

"I got a great one of the dog scowling at them. Did you see the dog?"

Matt noticed little dimples at the corners of her lips when she smiled. Enchanting. "Just a glance. I expect we'll be seeing more of him on TV and in the newspapers. He'll be famous for fifteen minutes—that's human time. What would that be in dog minutes?" Cathy blinked in confusion. "Dogs don't last as long as people," he added.

"Oh, I see what you mean." She felt a little awkward, talking to this quick-witted man. "I got quite a few good shots. A man walked right in front of me and spoiled one, but not the best one."

His interest quickened. So that was it! She had taken Carr's picture. That picture could be worth a million dollars to him—and to Carr. "That's too bad," he said.

"Oh, I got plenty of others." They had finished their first course, and looked at the menu.

Matt wanted that film, but he couldn't expect a policewoman to hand it over and leave it at that. She'd insist he notify the police. "Are you having dessert?" he asked while racking his brain for some means of getting the film without going into the whole convoluted tale of Jim Carr's crime. She wouldn't believe it, anyway. It was an outrageous story—a man faking his own death to dupe the insurance company. She already half thought he was trying to pick her up, and to enter into the Carr saga would reveal the tissue of lies he had told her.

"Just coffee for me."

They both ordered coffee. When the bill came, Matt reached out and took it. "Please, let me," he said.

Cathy, having foreseen this, already had her pen out. "You don't have to do that. I was happy to have your company," she said, and took out her hotel key to check the room number before signing the bill in a businesslike way. Matt glanced at the key number: 617. Then he took her jacket and helped her on with it.

"At least let me reciprocate and invite you to join my table for dinner," he said. Cathy gave him a knowing look.

"You can't blame a guy for trying," he said with an apologetic shrug.

She considered his offer a moment. She wouldn't normally accept a date with a total stranger, but they were both alone in a strange city, both Americans. It seemed to make it less questionable, and Matt seemed nice. "What did you have in mind?" she asked, arranging her shoulder bag over her shoulder.

"My own preference is for Italian. What's yours?"

"Chinese."

"Then it's all a hoax, that great minds think alike. I'm not adamant about eating pasta and garlic." He positioned his body to hide her camera, hanging on the back of her chair. Out of sight, out of mind.

Cathy had thought they might dine in her hotel, so that she would be on safe turf. "I don't think . . ."

He spoke eagerly before she could refuse. "Don't say no. You can always arrest me if I get out of line," he added facetiously.

"My favorite date. Arresting my escort!"

"Let me call you later, when you've had a chance to think about it." He put his hand on her elbow to lead her out of the coffee shop. "When will you be back in your room?"

Flustered, Cathy didn't give a single thought to the camera. "About five, I guess. I'm going to do some sight-seeing and photographing this afternoon."

"I'm hitting the art galleries myself. I'll call you at five. I'm really completely harmless, you know," he said with one of his charming, heart-swelling smiles. "I don't have a wife or a harem sequestered in Chicago. I'm not liv—er, involved with anyone at the moment." Oh, oh! That had been a mistake. He saw her eyes widen in surprise. Surely living with a woman wasn't shocking in this day and age? What was she, a nun? He hurried on to undo the harm of his thoughtless remark. "You wouldn't really have to arrest me, if that's what's bothering you. I don't molest women or drink too much. If you'd rather, we can eat right here in your hotel. That way, you won't have to be alone with me.''

This suggestion pleased Cathy, but she was a little taken aback by that casual ''not liv—'' Not living with anyone at the moment is what he started to say. ''I'll be waiting for your call at five, then,'' she said, and waved as she walked away. She was minutely aware that Matt was following her with his eyes. She had to force herself not to turn around to confirm it. This dinner date would take some thinking about. She was afraid Matt was a little fast for her. She'd go up to her room now and make sure her good dress was fit to be worn, anyway, just in case. It might have to be pressed after wearing it to the theater the night before.

As soon as she walked away, Matt returned to the table and got her camera. A glance was enough to tell him she had put in a new film. Through the little display window, he read Zero. So Cathy Auden had the film with the picture of Carr on it. It must be in her purse. He had followed her directly from the church to the hotel. She hadn't had time to go to her room. Maybe she was taking it out of her purse now, this very minute. He glanced at the camera—a good excuse to go to her room. And he now knew the number—617. With luck he could pocket the film when she wasn't looking. He headed toward the bank of elevators.

Jim Carr, watching the pantomime from behind the safety of a newspaper on a lounge sofa, smiled at this French farce. As he watched, one elevator door closed behind Wilson; the next car opened, and the woman in the red jacket came out. She walked rapidly to the coffee shop to inquire about her camera, but came out empty-handed. When she went to the desk, Carr moved silently up behind her with his sunglasses and tweed cap in place to hide his face.

''I'm Cathy Auden, in room 617,'' she said. ''I left a camera in the coffee shop, but it wasn't turned in there. If anyone leaves it at the desk, will you put it aside for me, please?''

Carr didn't have to stay within hearing range after that. He had just heard exactly what he wanted to know—her room number. If the film had been in the camera, Wilson would have removed it. He had just glanced at it and darted off. Carr looked at the big leather bag she wore over her shoulder, and grinned.

Cathy glanced around as she left the desk and noticed the man who had spoiled her shot at the wedding. She thought he must be a guest here, as he went to a sofa in the lobby and opened a newspaper. She returned to the coffee shop to ask if anyone had turned in her camera yet.

When she came out, Matt was just coming from the elevator, carrying her camera. ''Are you by any chance looking for this?'' he asked, handing it to her.

On the sofa the newspaper rustled with interest.

A wide smile of relief shone on Cathy's face. Matt was disturbed by the emerald sparkle of her eyes and the glinting of copper lights on her shiny hair. Such a nice woman—he hated deceiving her. She didn't seem so straitlaced for a cop. But what was the point of dragging her into all this unsavory mess? She was enjoying her holiday. And the company had demanded secrecy. Better to just get the film and leave her holiday undisturbed. He'd send her the pictures of Wolfe's wedding—anonymously—since she'd been so excited about them.

''Oh, you've got it! Thank heavens. I was afraid someone had stolen it on me,'' she exclaimed.

''Still intact, with your new film in place,'' Matt said.

Behind the paper Carr's face melted into a grin of relief.

''I don't know how I came to forget. I'm usually very methodical,'' Cathy said, shaking her head.

Matt decided he wasn't going to leave Cathy's side till he discovered what she'd done with the exposed film, not if he could help it. There was nothing he could do to find Carr that afternoon, anyway. "All set for more picture-taking? Why don't we go sight-seeing and picture-snapping together?"

His returning the camera told her that he was honest. Cathy felt an urge to accept his offer, but she had a tentative date with him that night and she really wanted to get those pictures for her parents' album. "You wouldn't want to go where I'm going."

"Try me," he suggested with a reckless little smile.

"I'm making an album for my parents' anniversary. I'm going to take pictures of their old house. It's in Etobicoke—wherever that is. I'll have to take a cab."

"I have a car," Matt tempted. "And a map. Etobicoke isn't that far away. It won't take long, and we can—"

"I'm planning on taking a picture of the hospital where I was born, too. It'd be boring for you, Matt, but I really want to do it. We'll get together this evening."

"I'd love to see where you were born," he insisted. "You can tell so much about a person by where she was born. I personally was delivered by a stork. That makes me a nice, innocent, old-fashioned sort of fellow, don't you think?"

"Wouldn't that make you a stork?" She laughed. He took her smile for acceptance. At least she didn't object when he put his hand on her elbow and led her out.

Jim Carr rose from the sofa and took the elevator up to the sixth floor.

Chapter Two

"I thought you had a car," Cathy reminded Matt when he hailed a cab in front of the hotel.

Laughter glinted in his smoky eyes, challenging her. "I do." As she looked from the cab back to Matt, his smile turned to a wicked grin. "A nice shiny new Corvette. It's at home. You wouldn't believe how unreasonable the airlines were about flying it from Chicago. They wanted a fortune."

"I mean I thought you had hired a car *here*, of course," she objected.

"That's what I'm going to do. And I plan to buy a map, too."

"You were lying, in other words," she charged, but she could hardly object to his ingenuity when he had done it all just to be with her. In fact, she could not quite suppress a small smile of approval.

"'Lying' is a hard word. You didn't ask where my car was. Is it my fault you assumed it was in Toronto? As to the map—I have a whole atlas at home, and a street map of Chicago, besides," he explained, all in a perfectly reasonable manner, but with an undertone of banter.

"That'll be a big help—if I ever go to Chicago."

Matt reached down to open the cab door. When his shoulder brushed Cathy's, their eyes were inches apart. The air between them crackled with electricity. There was a glint of amusement—or was it approval—in his look. "Be sure you call me, and I'll be there, map in hand, waiting to show my toddling town," he said. "Your hair smells lovely, by the way. What perfume is that?"

"It's just my herbal shampoo." For no reason she could readily ascertain, Cathy felt a thrill of excitement. There seemed to be a promise in his look, which caused something to stir in her. It felt like the beginning of an adventure. She liked the unpredictable way he hopped from the facetious to the intimate without warning. It kept her on her toes.

It's not just Matt, she told herself sternly. It's the beautiful spring day. Who wouldn't feel great with the sun so bright and winter over? And besides, she was on holiday. Matt held the door and they got in. He asked the driver to take them to the nearest rent-a-car office, which also supplied them with a map of the city.

"The house is on Woodward Avenue, in Etobicoke," she said, trying to establish a businesslike mood.

When they were in the rented car, Matt opened the map. It sprawled over their collective knees, taking up the whole width of the seat. She watched his long, shapely finger trace the column of street names. Once he had found the name, he located it so quickly on the map that Cathy felt he had a lot of experience in map reading. He checked the route, running a finger along the line and muttering to himself.

"I've got it," he said, refolding the fanlike length of paper with one hand.

"You're good at this," she complimented.

He flashed a quick grin at her. "I get lost a lot. Maps and I are old friends."

"Funny, you strike me as a man who knows exactly where he's going." And one who is sure everyone else will go along with you, if that's what you want, she added to herself.

"Thank you—I think. Or did I detect a note of mistrust there, as if where I was going was straight to the devil?"

"You're imagining things. It must be a guilty conscience." She shrugged. He didn't miss much!

He moved into the traffic and, after a false start, found his route to Etobicoke. It was an older area of the city, once a suburb before Toronto had grown up around it. The house on Woodward Avenue where Cathy's parents had lived was a small and by now rather run-down two-story brick building with a veranda and a patch of dispirited lawn.

"Why don't I take a snap of you in front of the house?" he suggested.

"I'll take one of the house first, then you take one of me in the yard," she decided. She lined up the shot, taking care to include the house number.

"Do you remember any of this?" he asked, waving at the street in general.

She gazed all around and shook her head. "Nothing. I was too young. Strange, isn't it, to think I spent three years of my life here, and I don't recognize a single thing. The only thing I remember is a sandbox in the backyard. A neighboring kid threw sand in my eyes once. I remember running to Mom, crying. I thought I was blind."

Matt gazed a moment at the wistful face, averted now, wondering how it had looked at three years. There was still a vulnerable, youthful air about her. "Nice neighbors," he said. "Want to try for a shot of the sandbox?"

"No, I'm doing this album for my parents' wedding anniversary. I'm not ready for nostalgia yet."

"That's a sweet thought, Cathy, taking these pictures for your parents. A present with thought and trouble is rare." In fact, he was beginning to think Cathy Auden was a rare person. Sweet, thoughtful, innocent. All the old virtues. But then, when your parents actually loved each other and stayed together for twenty-five years, you probably had a different view of life and marriage than he had.

"Well, since I'm here in Toronto..." she said dismissingly. "Shall we do the hospital next? Mom worked there, and I was born there, so that about finishes my itinerary."

"Which hospital?"

"The Wellesley General. It's closer to downtown. It should be on the map," she replied.

They found it with no trouble on the map. Getting there in the car was a little more troublesome, but eventually they stood in front of the sprawling hospital and again took one picture of the building, another of Cathy standing in front of it.

"Why don't I take one of you, Matt?" she suggested.

He dismissed this idea with a joke. "We wouldn't want to break your nice camera. And besides, my picture wouldn't have any significance for your parents—unless you have a long-lost brother?"

Cathy had every intention of getting a shot of Matt, but thought she could find a more interesting background and didn't insist. "Now it's your turn to choose our next stop," she said. "You mentioned seeing some art galleries. I'm no connoisseur, but I wouldn't mind being exposed to some culture."

"There's an interesting show at the Art Gallery of Ontario. It's a neat place. They have a whole collection of Henry Moore sculptures," he mentioned.

"Henry Moore," she repeated, frowning. "Is he the English sculptor who does those big, modern pieces—amorphous blobs that look like a melting snow-sculpture? The ones you see in cartoons, with a hole in the middle?'' she asked. "Sounds great."

"The *genius* who blends the human body and landscape into an art form," Matt replied, pretending to be shocked.

"Where does the hole come in?"

"The head, perhaps," he suggested, and took her arm to lead her back to the car. "You've heard of people with a hole in the head?"

"Uncultivated boors like me, you mean? Landscape is landscape, Matt, and people are people. I like Michelangelo's statues of people and I like Constable's landscapes. As far as I'm concerned, the two don't mix."

"Ah, a classicist," he smiled approvingly, but with a twinkle in his eyes. "Somehow that doesn't surprise me. Authoritarian, logically minded people usually are. They like to see all the rules obeyed, even in art, which is *supposed* to be a free, creative endeavor. You *do* know something about art. It's just that your interest stopped at the Renaissance."

"My interest stopped a little later, when art turned into a con game," she riposted. "It figures a stockbroker would like modern art."

"Look and learn," he said, and drove on to the gallery, where they argued for half an hour over the statues.

"Now, you can't say that's not a superb piece of work!" Matt said, pointing to a monumental statue that a discerning eye could see was a reclining lady.

Cathy found it impressive, but wasn't about to let him think he had influenced her opinion. "Your taste is all in your mouth. Her head's too small. And he gave her two little pinholes for eyes."

"He didn't want to disturb the smooth flow of the composition," Matt explained, gesturing to the curved mass of stone.

"He didn't want to bother carving her eyes, you mean," Cathy insisted. "I never found that David's eyes in Michelangelo's statue interfere with the flow of the composition."

His reply was in the mock-critic's style. "Your artistic education has been sorely neglected, my dear. I see I must take in in hand." He led her to the gallery's bookshop, where he bought her a book on Henry Moore, and led her off to some private galleries, where he spoke enthusiastically about the art. She liked that when he did a thing, he did it full power, with endless eagerness and energy.

"Why don't we take a picture of you in front of this one?" he suggested at the door of a small gallery on Bloor Street.

"Why don't I take one of you instead?" she parried. "We'll use your camera if you're afraid of breaking mine."

"Since I'm out of film, I left it in the car. I'm not photogenic. Say cheese." Matt was carrying her camera. He held it up, and she scowled. "Better get another one. Your eyes looked like the Henry Moore lady's in that one." He clicked again, wasting her film in Cathy's opinion.

They argued and laughed and talked and had a delightful afternoon becoming acquainted. "As you said, you don't know much about art, but you know what you like," he concluded.

"That is not what I said!"

He ignored her objection. "I bet I know what you'd like do to top off this day," he announced. "Shopping." Matt gave a satisfied smile when her eyes lit up in pleasure. "I knew that'd get you. The way to a man's heart may be via the stomach, but the way to a woman's is through the doors of a shopping mall."

"It's atavistic," she explained. "You may have noticed—animals stock up when they get the chance. Squirrels store nuts, camels store water."

"Storks don't store anything," he pointed out.

"No, they prey on smaller animals, don't they?"

He scowled in mock offense. "Actually I'm not a stork at all. I was left under a cabbage leaf."

"Oh, like a garden slug, you mean."

He tossed up his hands. "I give up. You're diverting me from my true point. Women store clothes, so let's go shopping. Shopping is the new hobby."

"It beats TV. At least it's real."

"No, it's a substitute for the lack of real meaning in our lives. People are trying to buy happiness."

"Yeah, look how well Adam and Eve did without any stores." She laughed. "Eve got so frustrated she had to steal."

"If you'd been there, you could have arrested her."

"Poor loser," she scoffed. "You're the one who suggested the shopping mall. You're also the one who did the shopping today. You bought the book and the map. I didn't buy anything."

"A scorekeeper, typical behavior of a classicist." He frowned, but there was a gleam of amusement in his smoke gray eyes. Why was she immune to his charm? At times he had the feeling Cathy was laughing at him. This was a new experience for Matt Wilson, and it intrigued him. She couldn't be entirely immune, or he wouldn't be with her now. She was just holding back. That must be it. He liked that restraint in a woman. He liked other things about her, too. She actually cared for her parents. She hadn't made any excuses about that modest house where she had been born. She was what she was; she liked what she liked, and no apologies. He was beginning to hope she liked him.

They drove to the Eaton Centre shopping mall and admired the fountains and geese sculptures suspended from the ceiling.

"Marvelous," Matt said, gazing up at the metal birds. They were arranged like a flock in flight, high in the vault of the mall.

"And they look exactly like geese, too. I bet they even have eyes," Cathy joked.

"Let me take a shot of you here, in woman's natural habitat, surrounded by stores," he retaliated.

"No more pictures of me, for heaven's sake. What do I want with all these pictures of myself?"

"You don't want them. I do. I hoped we could get this developed before we part."

She was flattered and suggested again that she take some pictures of him. "Sure, but let me get one of you with those geese in the background first. Okay?"

Matt found other locations he wanted to use for background—the fountain, a long shot of the area. As he handed her the camera, he noticed it was a good one. And she was using fast film, one-thousandth of a second. Even if Carr had just been passing in front of her, that fast film had probably gotten a recognizable shot of him. He knew his own shot would show the back of Carr, fleeing. It was always the way.

"That's enough," she said at last. "Now I want to take some of you."

He looked at the camera. "Too bad. That was the last shot." He took the film out and handed it to her. She opened her purse and slid the film into a side pocket. Matt saw the other film was still there.

His behavior was beginning to seem suspicious to Cathy. She wasn't in the habit of dissembling, and said, "Are you wanted by the police of something? Why wouldn't you let me take your picture?"

He blinked in astonishment. "I told you, I take a terrible picture. You'd wonder when you got home why you ever spoke to me. I'll look like a gargoyle. I always come out frowning. Now, where shall we get this developed? Ah, there's a kiosk right over there. You might as well get your other film developed, too, the one with Wolfe's wedding on it," he suggested casually. His heart pounded as he waited for her to draw out the other film.

"It won't be convenient, having to come back here. I'm going to get them developed at home." She saw the real chagrin on his face and wondered about it.

"I was hoping I could have some of these shots we took today," he said ruefully.

"I'll send you some if you like."

He just looked at her for a moment, disappointed. "You won't, you know," he said. "New acquaintances say things like that, and even mean it at the time. How often have you told people you met when traveling that you'd write, or they've told you? But did you ever really do it?"

"I'd do it, Matt. I do what I say I'll do," she said simply. "Why don't you give me one of your cards with your address?"

"I don't have any with me," he replied swiftly without even checking his wallet.

She looked at him and was struck with the knowledge that he was lying. He couldn't meet her eyes, and a light flush rose up from his collar. He was a terrible liar. He was ill at ease with this whole conversation, in fact, and it made her wonder. The first idea that occurred to her was that he was married, just enjoying a little fling while out of town. But if that were it, why would he want pictures of her? And she had even suggested his business card, which would put the pictures in his office, not his home, where his wife might intercept them. It didn't make sense.

His insisting that he wasn't photogenic was odd, too, when she considered it. He had agreed to having his picture taken when she goaded him, but that was just to disarm her suspicions. He'd taken care to use up all the film. There was definitely something very strange about this charming, mercurial man whom she had let pick her up. That's what it really amounted to. He had picked her up. She didn't know anything about him, except that he was fun to be with.

"Shall we go?" she asked curtly, arranging her camera and purse over her shoulder to avoid looking at him.

Matt didn't move, but just looked again at the photo hut. "I could pick the films up for you tomorrow," he said. "I'll get them and bring them to you at the hotel. I'd really like to see how these pictures come out."

"I'm not even sure I'll be here tomorrow. There's an early flight out in the morning, and I'll probably be on it."

Matt looked as if he wanted to object, but sensed that this wasn't the moment. He still had tonight to change her mind or get the film somehow. Conversation was desultory as they left the shopping mall. The day had lost its excitement for Cathy. She was sorry she'd said she'd see Matt that evening. At the hotel she'd tell him she'd changed her mind. Better wait till she was safe at the hotel. She realized that some part of her uneasiness was actually fear of the man beside her. She had had an uncomfortable feeling, off and on during the afternoon, that he was holding something back. It was part of what intrigued her.

What a fool she'd been to go out with a total stranger. Matt had almost certainly bribed that waiter to get a seat beside her in the coffee shop. Why? He didn't seem to be a sex maniac. Was he just lonesome? That didn't explain his wanting pictures of her. She shook away these webs of doubt and tried to smile. But smiles wouldn't come. She was behaving stupidly. If she didn't trust Matt, and she didn't, why should she get into his car with him again? She'd leave him now, here, and take a cab back to the hotel.

"It's early," he said. "Shall we grab a cocktail before we go to change for dinner?"

Whatever had been bothering him earlier, it had passed over now. Matt was his usual self—eager, friendly. A long evening alone loomed in front of her. The rest of the tour group had left. She didn't know anyone in Toronto, and if they had dinner at the hotel, nothing could happen. She hesitated. Had she been imagining things? It was foolish to take a chance.

"I don't think so, thanks. I'm going to have a little rest."

He accepted it easily. "I've tired you out with all the gallery hopping. Okay. What time shall I call for you?"

"I don't think—"

Before she could finish, he grabbed her hands. The handsome face gazing at her looked terribly earnest and sincere. "Cathy, don't say it. I really want to see you again."

"Why didn't you want me to take your picture, Matt? Who is it you're afraid will know we spent the day together?"

A look of confusion seized his face. "Is that what's bothering you? Good Lord!" He put his head back and laughed, then grabbed her hand. "Come on."

"Where are we going?"

"To have our pictures taken. There's got to be a machine here someplace. Four mug shots for two bucks."

They found an automatic machine, and Matt went in. She waited outside, wondering what this was all about. She saw the light go on behind the curtain, and in a few minutes Matt came out with the row of pictures. He'd made a grossly distorted face, gargoylelike, in the first. "I told you," he said, hunching his shoulders. The others were just normal pictures. He was smiling in two, serious in the last. And he handed the whole row to her.

"Let's pose together," he suggested, and they went, laughing, into the booth. They had to put their heads close together to both get in the shot. Matt hastily arranged the poses between flashes of the light. They posed, nose-to-nose in profile in one, like Eskimo kissing. In another, he took his tie and held it around both their necks. The warm touch of his cheek, the grazing hands and rubbing shoulders created an aura of intimacy that excited her. In the third they were laughing, not ready for the shot, but it was the best of the lot. And in the last he kissed her, just a light, disturbing touch on the lips that left a burning sensation out of all proportion to the actual physical contact.

She sensed the maleness of him in that enclosed space with their bodies touching. The clean sharp scent of soap, lightly spiced, emanated from him. His lips clung a moment after the light went out, causing a shiver along her scalp. Before the kiss could develop further, Cathy pulled away. He didn't try to stop her, but his eyes, in the shadows, held a hint of regret. In a moment the row of pictures spewed out of the machine.

"This one is mine," he said, gazing softly into her eyes, and ripped off the bottom picture.

The short curtain of the booth provided a very tentative privacy. He gave her a quick peck on the cheek before they left. She had her pictures of him now, so obviously he wasn't afraid of a camera. And he wasn't afraid of pictures of them together, either. That had been his idea. Cathy thought she must have been imagining things. Her mind was overloaded from the aftermath of her whole trip and her outing with Matt. He was a nice man, fun loving, amusing. What a fool she would have been to refuse to have dinner with him.

"Shall we have that drink now?" he asked. "Or are you really tired?"

"Just my legs. There's a bar on the top floor of my hotel. It looks out on the city."

"We can make dinner reservations at the hotel while we're there."

Cathy looked surprised. "I thought you wanted Italian."

"Just a whim. I think you'd prefer to be on your own turf?" His questioning eyes said the rest. You don't quite trust me—yet—but I can live with that.

"I wouldn't mind Italian tonight," she said to make up for not trusting him earlier.

"I'm just going to pick up a film while we're here," he said. Cathy went to the store with him. She noticed his camera took the same size film as hers.

When they reached the hotel, Matt asked, "Do you mind if I stop at the convenience shop to get a newspaper? I have a few stocks I want to check up on."

"Not at all. I'll get a magazine while we're there."

Matt picked up the daily paper, and while Cathy perused the magazines, he paid for his paper. He also broke open the roll of film he'd bought, to give the illusion the film had been exposed. He handed it to the clerk. "Put this in Cathy Auden's name, please," he said in a low voice. "It'll be ready by morning, I hope? Your sign says overnight development."

The clerk took it. "You're in time. Our films are picked up at six in the evening and returned at seven in the morning." She wrote out the receipt, which he quickly slid into his pocket. Cathy bought her fashion magazine, and they went to the elevators for the ride up to the penthouse bar.

Before choosing a seat, they went to the window wall, looking over the skyscrapers of the city. The stream of traffic below looked like toy cars on a toy road. The pedestrians might have been ants.

"I wonder if I could get used to living in a big city," Cathy said.

"They have their advantages, as well as problems. Where else would you have an institution like that?" he asked, pointing to a large gray building across the road.

"It's the Royal Ontario Museum, isn't it?"

"Yes, it has a world-class Egyptian collection, among other things. They're doing a show of Israeli art at the moment. I was there yesterday." As he described the exhibition to Cathy, his left hand hovered near the pocket of her red jacket. When his hand was in position, he released the stub for the film in her name. It fell into her pocket. "So, what'll you have to drink?" he asked, and took her elbow to lead her to a table.

"What are you having?" she asked.

No smile appeared on Matt's face, but he felt a smile glow inside. It was a beginner's question. He was glad she wasn't a sophisticated woman. "Beer for me. Same for you?"

She wrinkled her nose. "Beer tastes like tin. I'll have something tall and cold and sweet. A Tom Collins."

The after-work crowd began filtering into the bar, creating an interesting commotion. Cathy looked at them with pity. She felt luxuriously spoiled to be sitting at ease having a cocktail with a handsome escort after a cultural afternoon of sight-seeing. And that evening they'd be going out together.

"Shouldn't we make reservations for dinner?" she suggested.

"I'll do it as soon as we leave. Have you positively decided to leave tomorrow morning?"

Cathy took a slow sip of her drink, thinking about it. "I was originally going to stay till Sunday," she confessed. "I don't have to be back at work till Monday. I hoped some of the other tour members might be staying, too. I mean, it's not much fun alone in a strange city."

"You're not alone, Cathy." Their eyes met and held for a long moment. Words seemed to be spoken into the silence. "I'm here," he said.

"How long are you staying?"

"At least till the weekend. Not much fun being alone in a strange city," he said, repeating her words and looking at her hopefully. "There are lots of things we haven't done yet."

Why not take a chance? She had never met anyone like Matt before. She had a feeling she wasn't likely to in the future, either. The smile that peered up from the rim of her glass was uncertain. "My room's booked till Sunday. And my flight is for Sunday morning," she said.

"You may be here till Sunday, whether you want to be or not. It's not that easy to get a reservation."

"I guess I'll just have to make the best of it, then," she said, glad to have the decision made for her.

"I have a car and a map, and a newspaper now, to tell us what's on," Matt said encouragingly. He found he was looking forward to the next few days with pleasure, not just because of Carr, but because of this woman, this Cathy Auden. She was totally different from the women he usually dated. He wasn't strong on the idea of marriage. He'd seen enough of its shrapnel to fear it. Cathy would expect marriage, but certainly not after only a few days together. He could just enjoy her company, her friendship.

"You wanted to check your stocks, Matt. Go ahead. I hope they haven't gone down, or we might have to settle for hamburgers."

"I just sell them for my customers. I don't own them. But I'll see how my clients are doing." He made a pretense of checking the stocks, while Cathy began to think what she'd wear that evening.

Good Lord! In the excitement of leaving her camera in the coffee shop, she hadn't done anything about getting her dress pressed. She should do it at once. She quickly finished her drink, and said, "I have to go now, Matt." He stood up, surprised. "Don't leave your drink. I'll just take the elevator down to my room. What time will I see you tonight?"

"Eightish," he suggested.

It seemed rather late to Cathy. At home they had dinner at six. If they ate out, they went at seven, but in the city, of course, people were dining later every year. Eight gave her more time to see about her dress, so she didn't object. "Will you come to my room, or shall I meet you in the lobby, or what?" She felt uncertain at her lack of experience. There was probably a better way to handle this situation, but if so, she didn't know what it was and she didn't bother pretending she did.

"I'll come to your room. I don't want to leave you alone in the lobby, and in city traffic it's hard to be exactly on time."

"Eightish, then. Thanks for the drink. I mean—thanks for everything. It's been a swell afternoon." She stood up and began gathering her belongings, balancing book, magazine and purse.

"My pleasure." Matt stood up and handed her her camera. "You don't want to forget this—again."

She laughed, said "Bye," and left. Her mind roved over the unusual day as she went down to her room. The outcome of forgetting her camera the first time hadn't been so bad. If it weren't for that, her acquaintance with Matt would have been short-lived. She probably wouldn't have gone out with him. *Had* he asked the waiter to put him at her table? She'd ask him that night.

She entered her room and went immediately to the closet to examine the dress she wanted to wear. It was off-white, scooped in front, with long sleeves. The wrinkles had fallen out while it hung in the closet, but there was a little spot on the front where she had dropped a bit of strawberry juice at dinner. Maybe she could sponge it out. She took it into the bathroom and dampened a facecloth. With a bit of soap, she got the spot out. Now if the water didn't leave a mark, she was all set.

She hung the dress on the shower rack, then went to her bedroom to kick off her shoes and lie on the bed, perusing the Henry Moore book Matt had got her. Did he really like these great modern hunks of sculpture? They looked childish to her, but maybe that was because she didn't understand them. A mixture of the human form and landscape, Matt had said. Were the lumps in the picture she was looking at supposed to be hills or breasts?

Her mind wandered from the pictures, and she gave up any pretense of trying to understand Henry Moore. It was Matt Wilson she was interested in. He had asked the waiter to put him at her table—she was sure of it. Probably bribed him, as it didn't seem to be hotel policy. If she were more traveled, she probably would have objected to the imposition. And she wouldn't have been so flustered when she left that she forgot her camera.

How had she come to do it? She seemed to remember Matt was standing in front of it. Had he positioned himself there on purpose so she would forget it, giving him an excuse to see her again? That was probably it. He was certainly persistent. Why had he chosen her when Toronto was full of pretty women? Maybe it was love at first sight, like her parents.

She drew the row of pictures of Matt out of her purse to examine, asking herself if she could love him. It wouldn't be hard. The likenesses were very good for a photo machine. Why had he said he took a terrible picture? He took a wonderful picture, much better than she did. She looked really stupid in that shot with his tie around her neck. Her eyes looked ready to pop out of her head.

He had laughed at the idea of not wanting a photo-
graphic record of their acquaintance. These pictures proved
he didn't mind that. But he had definitely looked uncomfortable when she asked him for his business card. In fact,
he looked as if he weren't telling the truth. But he had
bought a newspaper to study the stock prices, so he must be
a stockbroker. Why would he lie about a silly thing like that?
If he weren't a stockbroker, he was obviously some kind of
respectable businessman.

Cathy looked at her watch. Five-fifteen. She wasn't
meeting Matt till eight. They wouldn't actually eat anything before eight-thirty. Over three hours. She'd never last.
She'd nip down to the little shop in the hotel and buy some
salted nuts to tide her over. She got her purse and went
downstairs, hoping she didn't meet Matt on his way out.
There was no sign of him. She picked up a bag of salted al-
monds and went to pay for them.

As the clerk was serving another customer, she had to
wait. The clerk looked at her. "More films to be developed?" she asked in a friendly way. Cathy had been in the
shop several times during her stay.

"I beg your pardon?"

"Do you have another film to be developed? The man
from Quick Developing picks them up at six."

"I didn't leave a film," Cathy said.

"The gentleman you were in here with a while ago left one
in your name. You're Miss Auden, aren't you?"

Cathy frowned in confusion. "Yes, I'm Miss Auden. I
just want these nuts," she said, handing the clerk the money.

The clerk checked her list. "We have a film in your name
going out with this consignment," she said. "You can pick
it up any time after seven tomorrow morning."

"The gentleman left it?" Cathy asked.

"Yes, but in your name. Perhaps he meant to ask you to
pick it up for him and forgot."

"That must be it," Cathy said. She accepted her change and left.

Her mind seethed with questions as she returned to her room. What film had Matt left? Had he smuggled her film from her purse and left it to be developed, since he was so eager to have her picture? She felt a stab of anger. As soon as she was in her room, she checked her purse to see if the film was gone. It was there, along with the film that had the pictures of Wolfe. Matt was strangely interested in films and pictures, one way or another. It was a skein running through the whole of their short relationship.

She tore open the bag of salted nuts and popped a few in her mouth to help her concentrate. There was something strange about Matt Wilson. And whatever it was, she meant to find out before she had anything more to do with him. She reached for the phone, then drew her hand back before she touched it. She didn't know where he was staying. Odd he hadn't mentioned the name of the hotel.

She'd ask him that night, anyway. It gave her an excuse to see him again, but there would be no Italian food, even if he had made a reservation. She wouldn't walk one step beyond the safety of the hotel till she had a good and logical explanation for everything.

She went into the bathroom to see if the damp spot on her dress was leaving a stain. If it was too slow in drying, she might have to use her hair dryer on it. From the corner of her eye, she noticed her cosmetics bag had been upset. The contents had spilled onto the counter. The maid must have done it. But everything else in the room looked almost unnaturally tidy. Surely the maid wouldn't have left her bag like that if she'd accidentally upset it.

Cathy went into the bedroom and looked around. Her suitcase rested on a rack at the end of her bed. She went to it and opened the lid. It hadn't been snapped shut, but she hadn't left it actually ajar as it was now, had she? She looked at the contents. They were jumbled into a heap, underwear and shirts all mussed up. She certainly hadn't left them like that! She planned to wear that green shirt tomorrow. As she took it out and folded it, her fingers were trembling.

It couldn't have been Matt. He was with her the whole time. Except before he joined her in the coffee shop.... Had he come here before he bribed the waiter to meet her? What was going on? Her heart was skipping fast with fright and curiosity, and anger. Whatever it was, Matt Wilson was certainly at the bottom of it, and she'd get an explanation before he left that evening.

Chapter Three

As she dressed for the evening, Cathy assured herself that the trouble she was taking to look good had nothing to do with Matt Wilson. She didn't plan to go out in the big city looking like a country mouse, that's all. She fussed with her hair in front of the mirror. She'd had it cut in a new style for the trip. It feathered back from her brow and hung in loose waves at chin length. The new shampoo she was trying added coppery highlights that winked in the mirror.

She brushed on a light film of pearly eye shadow and drew a feathered line around her eyes. Large and green, her eyes were her best feature. Summer had not yet tinted her face, so she applied a touch of rouge, then lipstick. She didn't usually wear much makeup; again she used the mental excuse of being in a city. But it wasn't the city she thought of as she examined herself in the mirror. It was the intriguing Matt Wilson.

The stain on her dress had disappeared without a trace. It was a party dress, but simply cut. The off-white color called for jewelry, and she attached a Victorian carved jade necklace, left to her by her grandmother. As she had no intention of leaving the hotel, she didn't bother with a jacket. At ten to eight Cathy was waiting impatiently for her watch to say five minutes to eight. She had decided it would be safer to meet Matt in the lobby. At six minutes to, she took a last look in the mirror before picking up her purse. Oh, darn it! She should have put her essentials in her evening bag. Her big tan shoulder bag looked out of place.

Before she had time to make the transfer, there was a tap at the door. She felt a spurt of fear, as if it might be a mugger. She had to remind herself she was a cop; she could handle herself. She strode to the door and took a quick look through the little peephole. It was Matt! He had said he'd call for her here, but he was six minutes early. It looked almost as if he knew she had planned to intercept him in the lobby. Did he have some reason for wanting to get into her room?

She put her eye to the hole again, but couldn't see anything. It was perfectly dark. She kept looking, and a glitter right at the little window, told her Matt had his eye to the peephole. Her heart leapt, and at that moment there was another tap at the door. "It's only me," he called, and stepped back. He waved and grinned. "I knew you were peeking."

Matt looked so carefree and undangerous, she felt foolish at what she had been imagining. This was probably another misunderstanding, like the pictures she had thought he didn't want taken of him. She opened the door and stepped out to forestall his stepping in.

"All set?" he asked.

"Ready and waiting. You're early," she said, heading toward the elevator. If it weren't for a different shirt, white with a wide blue stripe this time, Cathy would have thought

Matt hadn't changed, because he was still wearing a dark business suit.

"I hit a lull in the traffic," he explained.

"Where are you staying, Matt?" she asked. "Did you have to drive far?"

"Not far. I'm down on Front Street," he said vaguely.

Her suspicions were reactivated at once. Why didn't he tell her the hotel name? "The Westin?" she asked.

"No, the Royal York." It was like pulling teeth, but he had finally told her. It immediately popped into her head that he might not be telling the truth.

The elevator bumped to a stop, and the door opened. It was crowded, so they didn't resume talk until they got downstairs. This was going to be the tricky bit, telling him she didn't plan to eat anywhere but at this hotel.

"I couldn't get us reservations at La Scala," he said. "Old Angelo's is booked up, too. I hope you don't mind if we eat here."

She felt a wave of relief at one hurdle avoided. "It's fine with me."

He stopped in front of the directory. His fingers tightened on her elbow, and he looked deeply into her eyes. "I'm not really that fussy—about food," he said with a lazy, intimate smile. Her blood warmed at his flirtatious mood. His eyes suggested that it was the woman he was interested in, and he *was* fussy about that. His look also said that he found his companion more than satisfactory. It was going to be difficult taking Matt to account if he carried on like this.

"The food here is good," she said in a businesslike way. "Our tour group dinner was great."

Matt noticed that she was a little stiff, but didn't mention it. He had also noticed that she was careful not to let him into her room. Did Cathy suspect something? He mentally traced their steps, but couldn't see where he had slipped up. "You know the route to the dining room, then. Lead on."

They stopped at the doorway to wait for the maître d' to seat them. Cathy felt a sense of elation at the lovely setting. She had an impression of masses of flowers, of candlelight flashing and reflecting in mirrors. At eight the guests were just beginning to arrive. They were led to a table on the far side of the room. A hurricane-style candle lamp with a frosted globe cast a diffused glow on a vase of pink roses and baby's breath. It reminded Cathy of a bridal bouquet. The linen-covered table was already set with cutlery and glasses.

The sommelier brought a menu. "Do you want to choose the wine, Cathy?" Matt asked.

"I don't know much about wine," she admitted frankly. "Why don't you order?"

"Red or white?"

"White," she said. "Unless you're having a steak—" At least she knew that red wine was usually served with red meat, white with fowl and seafood.

"White's fine with me." He ordered a Chablis and settled comfortably in to talk while they waited for the wine. "Well, have you been studying up on modern sculpture?" he asked to get the conversation rolling.

"A little. I'm as confused as ever."

"It takes a while to get used to it. It's not that different from classical sculpture, really. The same principles of composition apply. It's just that the distinguishing body and facial characteristics are left out."

"The faces are what makes art interesting for me. I love those old Greek and Roman statues with stern faces. They always remind me of Dad."

"A stern moralist, is he?" Somehow that didn't surprise him.

"Well, he *is* a policeman, you know. A detective."

"And you plan to follow in his footsteps," he said, nodding. "I'll have to remember not to pocket any cutlery." He grinned.

"Yes, I'm always on the job. As a matter of fact, a few things about you intrigue me."

Matt looked up, startled. As she watched, his expression softened to flirtation. "I'm flattered! A great many things about you intrigue me, too. Mostly the eyes, I think."

She shook her head. "Compliments aren't going to work, Matt. Why did you leave a cartridge of film at the shop in my name?" She studied him closely for his reaction.

In the first confusion, Matt was grasping at straws and decided to disclaim it. "What? What film?" Her steady gaze seemed to bore straight into his brain. He saw her watching as he toyed nervously with his napkin.

"The one you left—in my name. Matt, what *is* it about pictures and cameras and films? They keep cropping up in our acquaintance."

"I'm not carrying one tonight," he said reasonably. No chance of getting a shot at night.

"I'm beginning to think it's my camera you like, not me! Did you bribe the waiter to put you at my table at noon?"

"You saw yourself the place was crowded."

"Yes, and I saw lots of other single people at tables for two. The waiter didn't seat anybody with them. You bribed him, didn't you?"

He hunched his shoulders and tossed up his hands to signal defeat. "All right, I'm guilty. I like you. I spotted you in there. I thought you were pretty. You were alone—I was alone. I gave him ten bucks."

Cathy was insensibly flattered, yet she felt there was more to the mystery than that. "But it wasn't just that you wanted to meet me. I think you hid my camera when I was leaving. And this afternoon you wouldn't let me take your picture, then suddenly you took a whole batch of them yourself. You looked as guilty as sin when I asked you for a business card and—''

Matt rubbed his hand over his chin, looked at Cathy and decided to bite the bullet. "You're right, I have some explaining to do. I could probably talk the rest of it away, but the film in your name—that one defeats my imagination.''

Cathy's eyes were like saucers. She waited with bated breath for what he had to say. She couldn't think of any possible explanation for all of this, but she felt in her heart it involved a woman and was resentful. She waited for him to continue.

"There's a man, Jim Carr, who's supposed to be dead,'' he said.

"A man! I was sure it would be a woman.'' She regretted that revealing remark, but Matt didn't take much notice of it.

"No, a man. I saw him today on Bloor Street. I was this close to nabbing him.'' He held up his finger and thumb, an inch apart. "I couldn't even get a picture of him. He was off like a rabbit when he realized he'd stumbled into a crew of photographers.''

Her look of surprise turned to delight as he watched. "You're a policeman, like Dad!'' she exclaimed. "Are you from the FBI?''

"I'm not a policeman, Cathy. No more lies. I'm an insurance investigator.''

Her hand flew to her lips, and at that moment the sommelier brought their wine and performed the ritual of pouring a sample for Matt to try. Eventually they each held a glass of wine, and the waiter left. "This man, Jim Carr,'' she said excitedly, "you said he was supposed to be dead. How is he supposed to have died?''

Before he could begin, another waiter appeared and they ordered dinner

When the waiter left, Matt began the story. "His alleged death took place in a sailing accident on Lake Michigan last October. A minor affair—you probably didn't read about it. He took a smallish boat out when the weather forecast was for storms. No crew. There were no other boats out to keep an eye on him. The boat had an engine, as well. It exploded—or was blown up. Carr's jacket with ID was recovered amid the debris. He wasn't a strong swimmer. He had taken out a five-hundred-thousand-dollar life insurance policy six months before, double indemnity in case of this sort of accident. I don't think he drowned."

"Why does he need so much money?" she asked.

The naiveté of her question, especially from a cop, surprised him. "Why do people rob banks and cook company books? He doesn't *need* it. He's just greedy and dishonest."

"I know what you mean." Cathy worried her lip a moment, and said, "I don't see how he could have survived the accident if there was a storm and he wasn't a strong swimmer."

"That's exactly what we're supposed to think. But why would an inexperienced sailor go out in such weather?"

"Maybe because he *was* inexperienced and didn't realize the danger," she suggested.

"He wasn't completely ignorant. He'd been taking lessons at a sailing club that summer. I think he rigged the motor with a bomb and a long-enough fuse to let him get safely away. I can't prove it. There were no witnesses, and only bits and pieces of debris were found by the time I was called in to investigate. No trace of the body ever showed up. I think he had a motor launch standing by and was long gone by the time the sailboat blew. In any case, I know he didn't perish, because I saw him today."

"Jim Carr," she said.

He nodded. "He dropped from the face of the earth for a few months, but I've been keeping an eye on his widow. She's made two trips to Atlantic City. She and Jim often used to go there, so it didn't look too suspicious. I went to Atlantic City and scouted around. She'd been seen with a man who could be Carr. He'd changed his hair color, of course, and wore disguises. They were careful, but I did get one pretty good clue." He took a sip of his wine.

"What was it, the clue?" she prodded impatiently.

"Carr has a cycle-shaped scar on his right thumb. I even know how he got it. He got his thumb stuck in a tin can when he was a kid and ripped it badly getting it out. A guy in Atlantic City remembered the scar. He'd played poker with Carr, several months after he was supposed to be dead. Carr has a penchant for gambling and covets fast cars. He also collects old silver. Not coins, but tea sets, salt cellars, bowls, that sort of thing. I've become an expert on Carr over the past months. He has a morbid fear of flying. He likes classical guitar and drinks vodka."

Cathy knew that in some way all this involved her, and said, "You said he'd changed his hair color. What color is it now?"

"It was white in Atlantic City. He wore a tweed cap pulled down quite low when I saw him today."

"Did he wear a tweed jacket and dark glasses?" she asked.

He nodded. "That's right. The guy who spoiled your shot of Wolfe's wedding."

Cathy felt weak. "His hair's hennaed," she said. "He lifted off his cap and apologized for ruining my picture."

"Yes, and he spotted me when he stopped. He hopped into a cab and got clean away. This is the closest I've managed to get to him. I followed him here from Atlantic City two weeks ago. He was calling himself Jack Connelly then. Earlier he was Jonathan Cullen. They often hang on to their initials, for some reason. A subconscious reluctance to give up their identity, I suppose."

"I have nothing to do with him, Matt, if that's why you've been chasing me." Cathy was aware of a feeling of letdown. Matt didn't care about her at all. She was just a cog in his detecting machine.

But when he looked up, his gentle smile told her she was wrong, and she felt an unexpected, dizzying jolt of joy. "That's not my only interest in you, Cathy. But you do have something to do with him. You have his face on your film, and with Wolfe's wedding in the background to give the date. If I can get a picture of Carr alive and well at this time, my company's off the hook for that million dollars."

"You mean they haven't paid the widow yet?" she demanded.

"These things take time, when the policy is so large and the circumstances are suspicious."

"Why didn't you just ask me for the film?" she asked simply.

"I thought of that, of course," he said, embarrassed. His whole ruse seemed shoddy and unnecessary with this frank and open woman. "There are a few reasons. In the first place, it wasn't certain by any means that you'd give it to me. I'm not a policeman—I could only ask, not order."

"I would gladly have given it to you for a good reason."

"Yes, I think you probably would, but I didn't know you then. In the second place, my work is secret. I blew a good opportunity in Atlantic City by telling a contact the truth. He went to Carr and warned him—for a good price, I'm sure."

"I hope you're not suggesting *I'd* do that!" she shot back angrily.

"I repeat, I didn't know you then. Now I'm sure you wouldn't." His smile went some way toward soothing her ruffled feathers. "The third reason is that I really didn't want to involve you in this whole unsavory mess. I hoped I could just get the film, and my proof, without revealing the rest of it. Since I've pretty well lost Carr's trail, that film is my last hope. At least he doesn't know who you are or where you're staying, so I don't think you're in any danger from him."

Cathy moistened her lips. She remembered seeing that tweed jacket at the registration desk when she was leaving the message about her lost camera. "He does know I'm here!" she said, and felt the bottom fall out of her stomach.

Matt's drink sloshed over the rim, and his body gave a leap of surprise. "What do you mean?"

"He was in the lobby right after we had lunch," she said, and explained when and where she had seen him. "He must have followed me, kept an eye on me from his taxi."

"Then he probably heard you give the clerk your name and room number," Matt said. "I was afraid something like this might happen. I didn't figure he'd trace you so soon." A worried frown pleated his brow. "You didn't leave the film in your room?"

"No, it was in my purse."

"Whew! That's a relief. I was pretty sure the film in your purse must have been it." She gave him a cool, appraising glance. "I happened to notice it this afternoon."

"I'm touched at your concern, Matt," she said tartly.

"You're in no danger. If he followed you, it's the film he's after. He isn't a murderer, you know."

"He may not be a murderer, but it's unsettling to know he can walk right into my hotel room and look around."

"What do you mean by that?" Fear for her safety lent a sharp edge to his words.

"I mean the person who had a snoop around my room today must have been Carr. I thought it was probably you," she added to repay him for his sharp tone.

Matt leapt six inches from his chair. "You didn't tell me someone had searched your room!"

"You're the last person I'd tell. I thought it was you! Except I didn't see when you had the opportunity, since you stuck like glue to my purse all afternoon." An angry look accompanied this charge.

"Cathy, I had no idea he'd followed you," he said, genuinely concerned. "If I had, I wouldn't have left you for a minute."

"You would have stuck by me in hopes of arresting Carr when he came calling for my film," she said ironically.

"It *is* my job, you know. I'm sorry. I really am."

"And another thing," she said, warming to the attack, "why did you leave a film in my name at the shop here?"

"How the devil did you find out about that?"

"I'm a cop," she boasted, although the discovery was purely accidental. "The question is, why?"

"It was foolish of me. I was trying to set a trap for Carr. It was a slim chance, but I thought he might be worried enough about that picture you took to nose around and see if he could find you. The place he'd look is where he first saw you, at that church, which is near to this hotel. If he happened to spot you coming in here, it wouldn't take him long to learn who you are and to get into your room. I—" he at least had the grace to blush "—I bought a cartridge of film, opened it so it wouldn't arouse the clerk's suspicions and planted the photo stub in the pocket of your red jacket on the off chance that he'd find you, and it. Presumably he'd recognize the red jacket you wore this morning and have the sense to search the pockets. He'd take the receipt and collect the film. And I'd be there to nab him."

Their dinner arrived, but by this time they had both lost interest in it. They just pecked at their food.

"And if I had happened to be wearing the jacket, then I assume I'd have to be knocked out. Thanks a lot, Matt," Cathy snipped.

"I was with you to be there if he showed up. And that's why I wanted to pick you up at your room tonight, to make sure you didn't wear it."

"I imagine that's also why you suddenly lost interest in eating Italian. So you could stick around the hotel."

"I booked in an hour ago," he admitted.

"I'm surprised you aren't letting on you did it so you can be near me."

"Two birds with one stone," he said with the culpable look of a boy stealing an apple. "Cathy, I really am damned sorry you're involved in all this. From now on we don't take any chances with your safety." The dark eyes examining her looked sincerely worried, but Cathy felt that Matt's main concern was Carr and the film.

"He's already searched my room. I don't imagine he'll be back."

"He might. You, your purse, your camera and your red jacket were gone when he searched before. He might have another go this evening."

Cathy blinked and turned rigid. "He might be there right now!" she exclaimed.

Matt put down his fork. She thought he was going to leave the table and run up to her room, but he just smiled and picked it up again. "You do have the film in your purse?"

"Yes."

"Then if he's there, he'll find the stub in your pocket, and when he goes to collect the film tomorrow morning, I'll be waiting for him. The guy brings the developed pictures at seven. I'll be on the lookout before that to make sure I don't miss Carr."

"Maybe Carr won't go to my room till later, like when I'm in bed, trying in vain to sleep, with all this on my mind," she said with an accusing look.

"You won't be in that room. You'll be in mine," he said calmly, and picked up his fork. Cathy gave him a startled look, but before she had time to object verbally, he added, "And I'll be in yours. We'll exchange rooms."

"You don't think it might occur to him that I don't wear men's suits and about size twelve loafers?"

"Size ten, actually," he countered. "My idea was that we'd leave your luggage and clothes there, except for your nightclothes and whatever you need. It would simplify things a whole lot if he *did* find that stub and steal it. I didn't think he'd find you so soon. He's a crafty scoundrel."

"It takes one to catch one," she said, and attacked her chicken with angry vigor.

"I hope you're not putting me in the same category as Carr! The man's a thief."

She thought about it a moment and realized that it was only disappointment and pique that were bothering her. With her parents' romantic past on her mind, she had been drawing some unlikely parallels. She had even indulged in a daydream or two that she and Matt might end up together, which was patently foolish. Matt had a job to do, and as a policewoman herself, she was the last one who would stand in the way of justice. She had a strong sense of responsibility and appreciated it in others. She became pensive and when she spoke, she spoke of something else entirely.

"Matt, why didn't you want me to take your picture today?"

"I just didn't want pictures of you and me floating around on the same film, that's all. In case Carr got hold of the wrong film somehow and learned that we were working together."

"He already knows it, or suspects, at least. He must have seen you when we met in the lobby and you gave me my camera."

"Yes," he said wearily. "Of course he knows. He was hiding behind a newspaper or something the whole time, laughing up his sleeve at me. We can't let you stay in your room tonight. We'll have to check into another one, registering under some new name. Who would you like to be?"

Mrs. Matt Wilson occurred to her, only to be rejected. "Some famous movie star," she said.

"A sexy actress?" He laughed, then turned serious. "Actually it would be better to put you up at a different hotel, just in case..."

Cathy felt the hair on her scalp lift. "I thought you said he wasn't dangerous."

"He's never attacked anyone, so far. If he thought he was in real danger of being found out, he might."

"I'll just take a room at this hotel under a different name," she decided. "I do have some training in self-defense, you know."

"Are you sure?" he asked. Cathy had the feeling he was happy with her decision.

"I'm not a policewoman for nothing. I have some interest in catching crooks, too, Matt."

Matt felt a spasm of apprehension. Here it comes, he thought. He'd have to fast-talk her out of it. "That's just to let me know I'm not the reason you're staying, right? I don't blame you. I haven't been exactly up front about all this, but there were extenuating circumstances. I hope you don't think I was just using you."

"You were," she said bluntly.

"No—well, maybe at first," he conceded. "But as soon as I met you, I wanted to spend some time with you to get to know you better. You're very—comfortable to be with," he said thoughtfully. "I wasn't doing much work on the case this afternoon. I just wanted to be with you. Actually I should have been out scouring hotels and apartments looking for Carr. You seduced me from the path of duty," he joked. "And that takes some doing."

"Sorry about that, but I'll make it up to you."

His dark eyes examined her with interest. "That sounds intriguing. What did you have in mind?"

"Helping you with the case, of course."

"No, really. I couldn't let you!"

"We have a good make on him, since you've been tailing him for months," she continued, as if he hadn't spoken. "He likes old silver. We'll hit the antique stores and see if a man fitting his description bought anything. If he paid with a credit card, and most people do, we'll have his address. Or if he paid with a traveler's check, we can follow up on that."

Matt's lips thinned. She spoke as if he were a rank amateur. "I've taken care of the rudiments," he said. "Carr usually pays cash. I think gambling is his main source of income. He avoids credit cards, understandably."

"Is he on any medications? The drugstores might provide a lead."

"No, he isn't."

"Any known associates?" He shook his head. "Did you check for traffic violations? The police might have something on him."

"I'd prefer to leave the police out of this," he said grimly.

"Why? That's what we're for!"

"Carr isn't wanted by the police. There are no formal charges levied against him."

"But we're interested in *preventing* crime, too. A formal charge isn't necessary—"

"I had something else in mind," he said hastily to divert her. Cathy's expression changed to one of inquiry. "He loves classical guitar. Serge Alceze is playing at the Royal York this week. That's the reason I originally booked in there. He opens tonight, playing Thursday through Saturday.''

She looked doubtful. "Shouldn't you stick around this hotel in case he tries to get into my room again?''

"If he gets into your room, Cathy, that'd be the answer to my prayers. He'd only do it to get that film. He'd take the stub from your pocket and he'd have to pick the film up, so that's as good as a rendezvous. My time will be better spent looking for him in case he *doesn't* risk going back to your room. And the best place to look for him tonight is at Alceze's concert. Do you like classical guitar?''

"It's all right," she said with a shrug. "I think it'd be better for one of us to wait here.''

"Why don't you stay here, then?'' he suggested reasonably.

This didn't satisfy her, either. The waiter came and removed their plates. "I bet I know what you'd like—cheesecake," Matt said, scanning the dessert menu.

"Yes, all those fattening things that aren't good for me. I'll have a look at the dessert table, please. And coffee.''

The waiter wheeled the trolley of French pastries to their table, and Cathy examined the delicious assortment. Puff pastries sprinkled with icing sugar and full of whipped cream, deep, dark chocolate glazes dribbled over some of them. Others had a center of glazed strawberries or cherries. Her mouth watered just to look at them. To choose one from this embarrassment of riches was difficult, but she finally chose a slice of chocolate torte. Matt chose the dullest thing on the tray, a piece of lemon pie.

"Sugar and spice are all very nice, but I also like a dash of tartness," he explained. His choice of quotation told her he was talking about women, as well as food. His eyes, lingering on her face, had begun to throw sparks that told her he meant her in particular.

Cathy felt again that stirring sense of promise and mentally scoffed at her stupidity. Matt didn't give a damn about her; he was just after Carr. He'd be just as happy if she stayed behind. Staking out her room wouldn't be much fun. And as Matt said, if he got the stub, he'd go after the film. It would be an exciting conclusion to her vacation to help him, and it would be great practice. She was impatient to become involved in a real case. She forced her mind to business. "I'll leave my red jacket in the room when we go to the Serge Alceze concert," she said.

"You've changed your mind about the concert, then?" She nodded. "Won't you want to wear your jacket? It's a bit chilly at night."

She was annoyed that he tried to sound concerned and gave a sharp reply. "A tailored jacket with this dress? P-lease. I'll wear a shawl."

"It's a very nice dress," he said in a voice of apology, "in case I didn't mention it earlier."

Her "thank you" was as stiff as starch.

They ate for a moment in silence. Matt knew she was peeved with him and as he examined their brief acquaintance, he acknowledged that she had every right to be. He really hadn't thought she was in any danger until now. It would be unconscionable to go on involving her now that Carr knew they were acquainted. She'd have the local cops involved before the night was over, too. Yet it would be nice to go to the concert with her.... He said reluctantly, "Cathy, I'm not sure this is a good idea. Let's just move you to another hotel, and I'll go to the concert alone."

She scowled. Now that he was finally showing some consideration for her, she resented it. Or she resented being left out, at least. "Two heads are better than one," she pointed out.

"No, really. There's no saying what Carr might do if he feared he was about to be caught. He's never carried a weapon before, but—"

"All right, Matt," she replied unconcernedly. "I'll go to the concert alone. If I happen to see Carr, I'll send a note to your table with the waiter."

He put down his fork and stared at her, his brows drawn together. "Why? Why are you doing this?"

"I'm in a mood to hear some classical guitar."

"I'll buy you a record."

"There's something to be said for the live performance," she said airily. His brows furrowed harder. "It's a free country, Matt. I'm going."

He drew a deep sigh and tried to look annoyed, but was aware of a bubble of pleasure. "Very well, but don't say I didn't warn you. It could be dangerous." Then he lifted his fork and resumed eating his lemon pie.

Cathy thought she detected a smile just before he opened his mouth. She realized she was smiling, too. She thought of telling Matt she wasn't completely unprotected. She had a can of Mace in her handbag. Since it was illegal, however, and since she was a policewoman, she didn't mention it.

Chapter Four

They checked Cathy's room before leaving the hotel. As the film stub was still in her pocket and the room showed no sign of having been searched, they assumed Carr hadn't visited her yet. Cathy picked up her fringed shawl, in case the evening air was cool, and they went downstairs.

"I took the hired car back," Matt mentioned. "A taxi's cheaper and more convenient than parking a car." They waited for the doorman to hail them a cab.

Matt, having regained his good humor over coffee, admitted to himself, if not to Cathy, that he was glad she insisted on going with him. The cab delivered them through the myriad twinkling lights and traffic of a city by night to the Royal York.

Cathy always felt a sense of exhilaration upon entering a fine hotel. Such occasions had been rare when she was growing up and still gave her a thrill. She felt as if she were entering a castle or a stately home of England when she went into the vast expanse of lobby. Her feet sank into the luxurious carpet. Overhead, monumental chandeliers of embossed crystal oblongs cast a welcoming glow on the busy lobby. She enjoyed the hustle and bustle and felt pampered by the general air of opulence.

A sign led them to the bar where Serge Alceze was performing. The room was dim and small enough to seem cozy. "More than a coterie, less than a crowd," Matt said, taking a close look all around the room. "Carr's not here yet. So much the better. It always amazes me that so few people take advantage of an opportunity like this to hear a world-class musician perform in an intimate setting. You can even sit close enough to watch his finger-work."

"There's a pretty good crowd, and people are still coming," Cathy pointed out.

"Yes, but the room hardly holds a hundred people."

"You're just afraid Carr will spot you too easily," she said. Matt led the way to a table in the darkest corner, with a view of the doorway.

The guitarist was just about to begin his first set. He came on stage, bowed, then arranged himself on a padded stool and took up his instrument. His first selection was an old crowd-pleaser, "Malaguena." From the opening ripple of golden chords, he held his audience in the palm of his hand. It seemed remarkable to Matt that a man could suggest a whole world with his elegant fingertips. He could almost feel the sultry heat of Spain and see the dark-eyed señoritas of Malaga flirting over their fans. He sat entranced, just flickering his gaze to the door at regular intervals. From the corner of his eye, he could see when newcomers arrived.

He spoke very little during the performance, but he did say to Cathy, "I wish we could sit closer to Alceze. I can't see his hands. I've taken up classical guitar myself as a hobby. I'd like to *see* him play, as well as hear him."

"He's on until Saturday. You can come back some night and sit closer." While Matt watched the stage, Cathy watched him. He seemed almost like a different person. His usual liveliness and energy were concentrated on listening. His face wore an air of absorption. At times his lips moved in silent appreciation of a particularly beautiful passage. His long fingers moved, too, as though the music possessed him. He remembered to watch the door, but it was obviously a nuisance for him.

"Relax and enjoy it, Matt. I'll watch for Carr," she said.

He reached out and squeezed her fingers in appreciation. "I usually work solo," he said, "but I could easily get used to working with you." He resumed watching, still holding her hand.

The number reached its climax in crescendo of strumming chords, and Matt led the clapping. "Isn't that incredible!" he exclaimed. "I have one thing to thank Jim Carr for—an appreciation of this kind of music. I've listened to a lot of it the past few months." He took her hand again after the clapping stopped. Cathy wondered if he even noticed he had done it.

"He's fantastic," she agreed.

After his dramatic opening, Serge played softer, romantic tunes. "This one is a Brazilian samba," Matt explained. "It has such a plaintive sound it makes me sad."

"I've heard it before. I'll let you wallow in it while I watch the door."

"Don't you like it?" he asked, astonished.

"It's beautiful, but business before pleasure." She was surprised and touched at this sentimental streak in him. His emotions were closer to the surface than she had thought.

The tune was followed by similar pieces, all sad and strangely moving, hinting at lost love and disappointment. The plangent music induced a reflective mood in Cathy. She noticed that Matt continued to be absorbed in it. His fingers moved over hers, unconsciously seeking reassurance from the sadness of the songs. When Serge rose and took his bow, there was a muted roar of applause. Looking around, Matt noticed that the room was crowded and gave a guilty start.

"Relax." She grinned. "He isn't here. With luck he's at the Park Plaza, pilfering that ticket from my red jacket."

"I don't usually get a chance to lose myself in the music. I really appreciate your help, Cathy."

"And to think, if you'd had your way, I wouldn't be here," she reminded him.

"If I had my way, we'd both be here, but not looking for Carr." His words, and the rueful look that accompanied them, were enough reward for her help.

Their glasses were empty, and Matt beckoned for the waiter, who nodded to show he'd seen them but was busy at another table. "Would you mind ordering when he comes? I really should dash out and make a phone call," Matt said.

"The same as before?"

"Yes, a beer for me, and whatever you want."

"Who are you calling? Or is that an indiscreet question?" It occurred to her for the first time that Matt might be involved with some woman back in Chicago.

"I was just going to call the Park Plaza and ask John—the house detective—if Carr has shown up yet. I spoke to him earlier. He's keeping an eye out for me. I told him not to interfere, but just to let me know if he showed. Carr isn't actively sought by the police, so John won't make an arrest."

"You could have him arrested for breaking and entering," she suggested.

"I'd like to have the pleasure of catching him myself. This has become a personal vendetta. If he takes the photo stub, he'll be at the coffee shop tomorrow morning to pick up the film. Anticipation is half the fun."

She looked doubtful. "A bird in the hand..."

"You're making me nervous with that kind of talk. Maybe we should go back to the hotel and wait for him."

"Make your call."

"Yes, boss."

He left and Cathy resumed watching the door. Matt had a bit of trouble working his way out of the bar. Quite a few people were leaving after the first set, and others were arriving. There was a throng at the door. She realized that plenty of newcomers had turned up while she and Matt had been talking, and began to scrutinize them carefully in case Carr had slipped in undetected. She was distracted again when the waiter came to take the order. He was friendly and talkative. "We haven't had a crowd like this in weeks," he said. "Toronto's a good city for music. You from Toronto?"

"No, I'm from the States."

"Buffalo, right? We get a lot of visitors from Buffalo. Well, it figures." The waiter picked up the empty glasses and wiped the table. "You must be with the dentists' convention."

"No, I'm just touring the city, actually. It's a special treat to hear Serge Alceze." She ordered the drinks, and he left.

Cathy resumed her interrupted study of the room. Several of the tables held new customers now. The three young men who had annoyed Matt by talking during the performance were gone, replaced by a quiet, older couple. The pretty blonde in the black dress and her escort were gone from the corner table. It was a bit hard to see who had replaced them. The table was across the room and dark, like her own corner. She leaned aside and peered at it. Just one man there alone, talking to another waiter. She waited until the waiter left, then unconcernedly glanced that way again. Her heart lurched in her chest.

It was hard to be sure, but the man could be Carr, and he was staring right at her! She sat, irresolute. If she left, he'd see her for sure. In this dim light, he might not be certain who she was. Anxiety gnawed at her. Should she go and tell Matt? But if she left, Carr would see her and skip out while she was looking for Matt. Oh, damn, why didn't Matt come back!

The waiter came with fresh drinks, momentarily blocking her view of the other corner table. She looked to the door to see if Matt was coming back, and saw a henna-colored head and a tweed jacket slipping out. The man held a newspaper at a strange angle, partially concealing his face, but she saw enough. It was Carr! She opened her wallet and handed a bill to the waiter. "Keep the change," she said, and darted out after Carr. He looked over his shoulder as he scampered down the hall, and saw her. That one sharp, angry look from his eyes chilled her blood. His hand moved to his pocket as if reaching for a gun.

He wasn't heading toward the lobby, which was strange. She thought he'd make a beeline for the front door, but he went off down a different corridor, tossing his newspaper onto a sofa as he went. She didn't follow him alone into the bowels of the hotel. It would be foolish to risk her life, but she retrieved the newspaper in case it might hold some clue. It was only one section of the paper. She folded it up and rammed it into her purse. She stopped a young man in hotel uniform to ask for directions to the closest phone, assuming Matt would be there. The man pointed down the hall, and as she looked, she saw Matt coming toward her. When he saw her, his face assumed a questioning, wary look, and his walk speeded up to a run.

"What happened?" he demanded. His voice was harsh with concern. His hands reached for hers and clutched at them as if to rescue her from danger.

"Carr was here and he left. That way!" She pulled her hand free and pointed to the corridor. Still holding each other by one hand, they ran after him. Her fear had vanished, and excitement took its place. Her high heels clattered on marble, making progress difficult, but Matt's hand steadied her.

"Did he recognize you?" Matt asked.

"Yes."

"Say anything?"

"Nope, just took to his heels."

They came to a staircase and saw before them another corridor with a bank of elevators. They stopped, looking right and left and all around. "This is hopeless. It's like looking for a needle in a haystack," Cathy said. "He could have gone up or down or out of the building entirely. I would have followed him, but I thought he was drawing a weapon."

"I'm glad you didn't!"

"What did the house detective you called have to say?"

"Carr was at the Plaza, all right, about an hour ago. John didn't see him enter, but he spotted him as he left. I asked John to check your red jacket. The film stub is gone." They exchanged a smile of triumph.

"So he'll pick the film up tomorrow morning," she said.

"Unless seeing us here tonight puts him off."

"He didn't see *you,* Matt. I was alone when he saw me. He can't know for sure that we're working together."

"Let's go some place quiet to talk," Matt said. "There's a coffee shop downstairs. Oh, I should go back and pay for our drinks."

"I took care of it."

He lifted his eyebrows in compliment. "You really keep your head in an emergency. We'll settle up later. Let's go."

They went down to the coffee shop and ordered a cup of coffee to give them an excuse to sit down in private. "He might have seen me as I was leaving," Matt said, worried. "I don't know why else he would have run off like that. He has no reason to be afraid of you."

"That's true."

"If he's really frightened, he might not show up to claim that film."

Cathy thought about it for a moment before speaking. "His reaction could have been a guilty conscience if he'd just broken into my room. If the picture means a million dollars to him, he'll show up. I bet he'll be there at the dot of seven, thinking to claim it before we're looking out for him."

Matt shook his head doubtfully. "He knows me better than that. He knows I'll be there."

"Yes, but think, Matt. He doesn't know you know that stub was in my pocket. If he's seen us together, he's probably figured out that you're trying to get the film from me, but he might think you're doing it without informing me."

Matt rubbed a thoughtful hand over his chin. "That's possible. Or he might send someone to pick it up for him, in which case we follow the man to Carr. I'll have to be there anyway, in case. That film is our ace in the hole. If it weren't for that, he'd be out of this city long ago. The fact that he's sticking around, when he knows I'm here, tells me he's plenty worried about it. I'll speak to the cashier and arrange for her to give me a signal if anyone asks for your film."

"Then you can relax till seven o'clock tomorrow morning. Shall we call it a night?"

Matt gave an apologetic smile and reached for her fingers. "This is some good time I'm showing you, Cathy. I didn't mean to involve you in all this business. When it's over, we'll go out and paint the town red, whether I catch him or not. A six-course dinner at the best Chinese restaurant in town."

"We'll see. Meanwhile, there's no point my changing rooms, is there? Carr got what he was after. He has no reason to come back."

"He didn't really get what he was after," he pointed out. "He got a stub for an unexposed film, but he won't know that till morning, so you're safe tonight. When he discovers his mistake, he'll go after the real film. Maybe you should give it to me for safekeeping."

"Is it any safer with you? He's likely seen you, too."

"Is it in your purse?"

"Yes, it's busily burning a hole there. Why?" Matt just sat, thinking, wondering what was safest for Cathy and most helpful to the case. "The safest thing to do would be to put it in an envelope and mail it to your company," she said.

"That's a good idea," he said, but perfunctorily.

"So, let's do it."

"The thing is, I'm dying to know if your shot of him turned out. If it did, then the case is half-solved. I have proof he's alive. I can turn the matter over to the police and let them find him. A bit of an anticlimax after chasing the crook for eight months, but it's the sensible course."

"Your company can get it developed and phone you."

"Ye-e-e-s," he agreed, still dissatisfied. "But that'd take a few days. I'd like to know *now*. Because if the picture *doesn't* turn out, I've got to get cracking and find him before he hops a boat to Rio or Bermuda, or a train back to the States."

Cathy thought it over, and said, "What we need is the yellow pages, to find a twenty-four-hour film developing lab."

That brought a smile to his face. "Two minds that speak as one. Back to the telephones."

They finished their coffee and went to the phone stalls in the hotel. There was a long list of photo development firms. They passed over the large commercial establishments and automated photo labs that kept regular business hours.

"Here's one," Matt said. "Discreet work, twenty-four-hour service. Reasonable rates."

"Discretion, that's what we want. How did they know?" Matt was curious at the knowing tone of her voice. "These places cater to people who have been taking naughty pictures of each other and are ashamed to send them to a commercial outfit," she explained.

"Fancy a nice woman like you knowing that, Ms. Auden. Candid shots, huh? Nudge, nudge, wink, wink. I'm shocked at you."

"Well, I *am* educated to deal with the seamy side of life."

"Aren't these places against the law?"

"Let's deal with one criminal at a time. Now, what is the address here? Montague Street. How Shakespearean. Wherefore art thou, Montague Street? Better get out your map, Matt."

"We'll take a cab, but first I'll give the place a call and see if it's been closed down." Matt made the call. "He's still in business. Let's go."

They took a cab to a small side street not far from downtown. It had obviously once been residential, but was now commercial, not regular retail outlets, but small shops selling such things as vintage comic books, stamps and coins. "I don't see number eleven," the cabdriver said as he coasted slowly along the dark street.

"It's eleven A, actually," Matt reminded him.

"There's eleven, but you can see it's black as pitch. The guy sells war memorabilia—WWII. Medals, uniforms, that kind of stuff. There's a driveway. Some of these places have turned the garage into a house or shop. Apartments are as scarce as dogs' feathers. Want I should wait?"

"We may be some time. Thanks, anyway." Matt paid him and they got out.

A sense of menace closed around them as they left the lighted street and crept along the shadowy graveled driveway, clutching each other's hands for comfort. They continued toward a building with a light in the window. At close range the building showed itself to be a clapboard garage with a second story added. The original door, large enough to accommodate a car, had been removed and replaced by a regular door. A sign on it proclaimed Discreet Developing. Matt knocked and a man answered immediately.

He had long red hair, a red beard and mustache and wore granny glasses. Faded and torn jeans, a blue shirt and sandals completed the picture. "You the guy that phoned?" he asked, examining them suspiciously.

"That's right," Matt replied. "I have a film here I want processed in a hurry. I only need one picture developed, however."

"A hundred bucks."

"A hundred bucks! That's highway robbery!" Cathy exclaimed.

"I have to make negatives of the whole film before we see which one you want developed. Englargements extra."

"We won't require any enlargements," Matt said, stepping in. "Just do it as quickly as you can."

The place was used as a residence, as well as a shop. The man, he called himself Judge, took the film and invited them to make themselves at home. "It'll take a while," he said. "You can't hurry the process."

Cathy looked around and felt she had entered a time warp. It was the sixties revisited, with psychedelic posters, more cushions than furniture and some amateurish ceramic pottery jostling for space with books on the row of shelves. The echo of folk music came from the next room.

"This'll take a while," Judge repeated. "You can leave and come back in an hour or so if you like."

"We'll stay," Matt said. "We're in a hurry."

"Suit yourself." Judge left, and they looked about the room, ending up at the bookshelves. The books were mostly biographies of the rock stars of the sixties and seventies. Cathy selected a book on the Beatles, Matt one on the Woodstock Festival, and they settled down on the cushions to wait.

"I hope he does a good job on the film," Matt said in a worried tone.

"Why wouldn't he?"

They flipped through their books while one folk tune was followed by another in the next room. After what seemed an eternity, Judge came back with a row of negatives. "Hey, you were at Wolfe's wedding! Cool. Which one do you want a print of?"

Matt took the strip and held it up to the light. A smile of satisfaction curved his lips. It looked like a good, clear shot of Carr. "This one," he said, pointing to it.

Judge took it and examined it at the light. "You kidding me, man? That's the worst one."

"That's the one we want. Oh, and would you make three or four copies?"

"You sure? This one with the dog—"

"Quite sure."

Judge shook his head in bewilderment. "It's your dollar. How many prints do you want? Three or four? I'll throw them in for the hundred bucks."

"That's very generous of you," Matt said ironically. "In that case, we'll have four."

Judge disappeared. After another interval that seemed longer than before, they finally heard shuffling steps.

"Here come de judge," Cathy whispered.

Judge was back, holding the prints by the corner. "Here you are. Who's the guy? I don't even recognize him."

"He's not a celebrity. He's a criminal," Matt said, and took the pictures.

The effect of this speech on Judge was alarming. His eyes widened behind his granny glasses, and his face blanched. "Are you the fuzz?"

"Your sins are safe with me, Judge." Matt examined the picture with satisfaction. It was perfectly clear, and enough of the background was also clear to establish the setting and thus a date. "I don't suppose you take credit cards?"

Judge grunted. "You're putting me on."

"Yes, well, let's see what we have." He opened his wallet. By using some American money, he was able to come up with a hundred dollars.

Judge pocketed it and said, "If you don't mind my asking, why'd you bring your film here? I mean, there was nothing on it that you couldn't have gotten done at a regular photo lab."

"We were in a hurry."

"You should have gone to Charlie's place, just down the street. He has twenty-four-hour service. He would have done it for twenty bucks."

Matt and Cathy exchanged a look of frustration. "Thanks for the tip, Judge," Matt said. "Next time."

"Can I have my negatives, please?" Cathy said. "I want those pictures of Wolfe."

"Sure." Judge left and came back with the negatives in an envelope and handed them to Matt, but it was Cathy whom he was looking at. He examined her from head to toe in a way that gave her goose bumps. Then he turned to Matt. "I specialize in *personal* portraits," he said with a meaningful stare. "Any time you have some private shots of your girlfriend that you'd like developed, bring them along. I develop anything. No questions asked. And I'm very discreet. You don't have to worry that I'll keep any prints or sell them. Know what I mean?"

"Yes, I believe I get your gist." Matt's lips moved unsteadily. "Interested, Cathy?"

"Not tonight. I have a headache."

Judge accompanied them to the door and called after them, "Any time you have some special film to develop, I'll be glad to do it for you."

"Thanks, Judge." When they were beyond hearing distance, Matt added, "Girlie magazines are cheaper. And you don't have to wait so long. Of course, they lack that personal touch," he added with a wicked grin.

"I'm sure they make up in fullness of figure what they lack in the personal experience."

"I don't see any lack of fullness in your figure. Just right, I'd say." He put one arm around her playfully and pulled her against his side.

"The man has put ideas in your head," she said, disengaging herself. And Matt was putting ideas in her head. That hug felt good. "We're working, remember?" They continued their walk.

"All work and no play—" He slanted a questioning look down at her as he extended his arm to embrace her.

She stepped aside, deftly avoiding it. "What are you going to do with the pictures of Carr?"

Matt accepted his rebuttal like a gentleman. They reached the curb and waited to hail a passing cab. "Send a couple to my company. Keep one for a souvenir. And give you one."

"Me? I don't especially want one."

"But if Mr. Carr catches you in some dark alley, what he'll be after is the picture. If you give it to him, he'll leave you alone."

Cathy felt cold fingers tiptoeing up her spine at the picture this conjured up. "He'll want the negative, too."

"Give it to him. I'm going to get these in the mail as soon as we get back to the hotel."

They walked down to Carlton Street and caught a cab. "They have stationery in the rooms. You can address your envelope there," Cathy said.

"Yes."

She thought he seemed rather depressed for someone who had just gotten exactly what he wanted. She felt a little down herself. The adventure was over, or could be. "It's too bad you had to pay so much to get the film developed."

"I'm on an expense account," he said listlessly.

"Will you be going back to Chicago tomorrow?"

"I'll get hold of John, or the house detective on daytime duty, and try to nab Carr when he goes after the film tomorrow morning."

"It doesn't really matter if he gets away. You have your picture now. That proves he's alive."

"Yes, but I'd like to get Carr personally. He's outwitted me a couple of times. I'd like to wrap the case up neatly, with Carr in prison, where he belongs, not out walking the streets. Besides," he added, turning to her, "it gives me an excuse to stay here with you. I promised you a blowout when we got him. Paint the town red."

"You don't have to do that, Matt. It was good practice for me. I enjoyed it."

Matt looked a little hurt at her lack of eagerness. "I want to do it. This is as much your success as mine. You took the picture. I'll see if I can wring a reward out of the company for you."

"That'd be nice," she said, but the greater reward was his obvious eagerness to see her again.

After Matt had registered for a room, they went to Cathy's room to see if Carr had left any clues behind or done any damage. "I'd never know he'd been here if it weren't for the stub missing from my jacket," Cathy said after looking around. "He was messier the first time."

"This time he knew what he was looking for and where to find it. He knew you'd been wearing that red jacket."

"Why don't you get that picture ready for mailing? The envelopes and paper are in the desk."

Matt pulled out the pictures and examined them carefully under the light. Cathy went to his side to look at them. Matt put an arm around her waist. She thought he didn't even realize he was doing it, but it felt good. "It's too bad that tree is casting a shadow on the left side of his face," she said. "I mean, he's recognizable, but is it a good enough picture to definitely establish it's Carr?" she asked uncertainly.

"I've been asking myself the same thing. When a million dollars is riding on it, it has to be a positive identification."

"They say everyone has a double. That funny little cap he wears is sort of shadowing his eyes, too. Not completely, but on one side. The mouth is definitely his. He has thin, mean lips."

They exchanged a questioning look. "It does cast the shadow of a doubt," he admitted. "Of course, his wife will swear up and down it doesn't look a thing like him."

"Her word against yours."

Matt drew a deep, weary sigh and removed his arm. He began pacing up and down the room. "It helps. It definitely helps. It'll allow the company to delay payment, but it would be much better if I could hand Carr over to them in person."

"Which you will, hopefully tomorrow at seven."

"I'll mail this off to Chicago, anyway," he said, and wrote a short note to enclose with two copies of the picture. He gave Cathy one picture and the negative, and put one in his own wallet.

"I'll have to cash a traveler's check tomorrow and repay you for that round of drinks," he said as he returned his wallet to his pocket.

Cathy opened her purse to put her picture of Carr away. Then she saw the folded section of newspaper Carr had tossed away when she'd chased him through the Royal York. "Carr dropped this when he fled down the corridor."

He had folded it in four, for easier reading. Cathy went to the light and examined it, curious to see what a man like Carr took an interest in. It was the classified pages. One item was circled.

"Take a look at this, Matt," she said, and he joined her. "Carr has circled an ad for an antique show at Harbourfront on Saturday. If anything happens and he slips away from you tomorrow, we might find him there."

"He won't get away," Matt said through clenched teeth.

She gave him a sapient look. "Famous last words."

"That's enough about Carr for one night," he said, slipping an arm around her waist. This time she knew he realized he was doing it. His glowing eyes left no doubt of that. They were looking at her in a questioning way, asking permission.

Until that moment it hadn't seemed to matter that she was alone with Matt in her bedroom. In fact, she had invited him up and she began to fear he had misinterpreted her reason. The glitter in his eyes, and his anticipatory smile, told her what was on his mind. She used her purse as an excuse to move away from him. She walked casually to the desk to put it down. Matt followed her.

"I guess it's time to call it a night," she said, a little breathless.

He glanced at his watch. "It's early." His hands came out and rested lightly on her shoulders. She took it for the beginning of a good-night kiss and didn't move away, though she felt herself stiffen. His hands left her shoulders to move lightly down her body, tracing the outline of her curves. When he reached her waist, his palms opened wide and gripped her. He moved her closer to him while his eyes held her mesmerized. She felt hypnotized by their glitter.

His head came down, and his lips brushed hers gently. Then he lifted his head and smiled softly from those pearly gray eyes, which looked darker at night. She held herself tense, waiting for the kiss. It wasn't what she expected. His warm lips sought her throat, with his head angled in against her shoulder. The tantalizing warmth of his lips, rough yet soft, caressed her in a sliding movement from ear to collarbone. A ripple of pleasure ascended her spinal column, lifting the hairs on the back of her neck. At this close range she noticed a spicy scent coming from his hair. Their mingled breath hung suspended in the silent room.

His lips continued to browse appreciatively, lingeringly, turning her insides to hot mush. His cheek lay warmly familiar against her skin—taut, muscular, masculine. For an absorbed second she opened herself to the moment, enjoying the unusual intimacy of his lips. She raised her arms and placed them lightly around his waist, but loosely, ready to push him away if he got out of control. When she felt a moist flicker at the depression of her collarbone, she tensed involuntarily, then tried to move away. "All finished, Matt?" she asked. Her voice was unsteady.

He lifted his head and smiled down at her, a peculiarly intimate smile, as though they shared some joke. "We've just begun," he said, tightening his arms till she was crushed against him. The tender agony of his body pressing hers left a wordless longing, as of some pleasure too long denied.

She uttered a low sigh just before his lips seized hers. A storm of feeling inundated her as the kiss lengthened and deepened to a heart-pounding intensity that left her weak. When she felt his thumbs stroking her jaw with a possessive touch, she realized he was no longer holding her, except by emotional persuasion. She was pressing herself against him willingly, and his warm, hard body was encouraging her. It moved in a sensuous rhythm that accelerated gradually until her whole body throbbed with an immense need. A soft, growling moan echoed from Matt's throat, telling her that he felt it, too.

Cathy had never believed the theory that people "got carried away," but she saw now that she'd been too hard on them. She felt carried away, beyond the sane world of thinking and acting rationally. All that mattered was this explosion that was occurring inside her, and all she wanted was to be carried away completely. A pressure was building up inside her, and her breaths were coming in shallow gasps.

Matt slowly lifted his head. When she opened her eyes, he was gazing at her almost sadly. His lips moved to her temple, and he murmured against it, "Now I have something else to thank Carr for. *You*." And if I don't get out of here very quickly, he added to himself, Carr is going to have a ravishment on his conscience. He placed one quick, light kiss on her lips and moved away.

When he spoke, his tone was breezy, though his voice was not completely steady. "I'll call for you at seven hundred hours. That's 7:00 a.m., eastern time. Better make it ten minutes before."

Still in a daze, Cathy tried to concentrate and figure out what he was talking about. Carr, the film. "I'll meet you downstairs," she replied.

He just shook his head while gazing at her in a bemused way. "We'll go together. I don't want anything to happen to you." A slow grin spread across his lips, and he added, "That—in case you're wondering—is why I'm leaving now, most reluctantly. Make sure you lock the door after me. My room number's 609. If you hear any suspicious fumblings at your door in the dead of night, don't hesitate to call me."

"You've giving me the heebie-jeebies, Matt," she scolded, happy for the distraction. Yet she wondered how he could move so glibly from high-powered lovemaking to business. Obviously Matt wasn't one of those people who "got carried away" by the thrill of the moment.

"I won't tell you what you're giving me, but I'll provide you a little clue. If you hear a shower running, it will be in my room, and the water will be an icy jet. Maybe I'll stop off by the soft-drink machine and pick up a bucket of ice."

"Or you could ring down to the desk and see if they have a psychiatrist on staff," she suggested demurely.

He cocked his head to one side and examined her. "You consider love a form of madness, do you? Not much logic to it, I suppose. I was just trying to convince myself it was sane. So much for the theory that men and women aren't that different." He went to the door and opened it. "Don't forget to lock this and put on the chain." Then he opened the door and was gone.

Cathy checked the lock and put on the chain, but she wasn't really afraid Carr would come. She was still reeling from that word "love," tossed so casually into the air, almost as an afterthought.

Matt, in his room, was reeling, too. He had felt strong physical urges before, but never with a policewoman. Talk about oil and water! Yet she wasn't as hidebound as most of them. She had a certain flair, like taking the film to Judge. A policewoman wouldn't be as innocent as he'd been imagining. Not that he intended to try anything. He not only wanted Cathy; he respected her, too. It wouldn't do to go falling in love with a cop.

Chapter Five

Cathy had been staying at the hotel for a few days. She had slept soundly the night before, so she couldn't reasonably blame her lack of sleep on being in a strange bed. It was thinking about Matt Wilson that kept her tossing and turning for an hour. Was it really possible she had known him for less than twenty-four hours? Closer to twelve, actually. Half a day. She felt she had known him for years. Of course, since noon they had been together almost constantly, and under such unusual circumstances that he revealed more of his character than a man might ordinarily do in a whole month of casual dating.

She had already observed his good looks and debonair charm at lunch. She knew better than to judge a book by its cover, however, and thought about his behavior. She knew he could be an amusing companion, that he was intelligent and very determined. His following Carr proved the determination. And now she knew that he was a skillful lover, who prattled about love on the first kiss. She didn't count that little peck on the lips in the photo booth. In the darkness she smiled, remembering the photo booth.

What she didn't know was what kind of love he was talking about, but she had never heard of a cold shower curing real love. He had lived with one or more women, obviously. "I'm not liv—er, involved with anyone at the moment." It made his liaisons seem awfully impermanent. There was plenty of sexual attraction between them, but to Cathy love meant the sort of long-lasting devotion her parents had found, or created. Would a few more days be enough to nurture sexual attraction into her kind of love? She had still not reached any conclusion when her eyelids drooped closed and she slept.

She had set her traveling alarm clock for six-thirty. At a quarter to seven in the morning, she was up and dressed in an outfit that would allow her freedom of movement, in case chasing Jim Carr formed a part of her day. She wore tan slacks, a checked shirt, a light windbreaker and the sneakers she'd brought along for sight-seeing. Now if I only had a cup of coffee, she thought as she ran a brush through her hair and applied a daub of lipstick.

She was interrupted by a tap at the door. "Room service," Matt's voice called. Glancing at the mirror, she saw she was smiling. What foolishness was he up to now? she wondered. As soon as she opened the door, he handed her a disposable cup of coffee. He examined her from head to toe, not in an insultingly blatant manner, but in a hasty, head-to-toe appraisal that she figured didn't miss much.

"Good morning. I see you're dressed for the chase," he said approvingly as he stepped in.

"You, too."

Matt looked more relaxed than the day before. He wore a casual golfing shirt, chinos and a brown distressed leather bomber-style jacket. The turned-up collar gave him an air of casual elegance. She noticed he had switched to sneakers as well.

"Here," he said, handing her the coffee. "I figured if I was getting you out of bed at the crack of dawn, the least I could do was bring coffee. The coffee shop wasn't really open, or I'd have a Danish to go with it. I sweet-talked the lady in charge into providing the coffee."

"Strong-armed her, you mean," she joked, but accepted it gratefully.

His eyes twinkled in amusement. "You have the wrong part of the anatomy, and the wrong technique. I glad-handed her into it, with my glibly superficial charm and five Yankee dollars. I'm out of Canadian money. Have to do something about that as soon as we catch Carr. Skoal." He touched his cup to hers and took a sip.

"Maybe we should take our coffee downstairs and have it while we wait for Carr to come."

"Eagerness, that's what I like in my colleagues—and my ladies," he added with a grin. He watched her warily, wondering how she'd respond to that taunt.

Cathy noticed that "ladies," plural, but decided to ignore it. Why give him the satisfaction of knowing she cared? "I'll get my purse," she said. As soon as she had snatched it from the dresser, they left. Within minutes they were installed on the sofa closest to the hotel convenience shop, shielded by a spreading palm. Matt had a word with the daytime detective, who was lurking behind a plant with a newspaper shielding his face. When Matt returned, it was five to seven and the place wasn't open yet.

"John Reilly will make the arrest," he said matter-of-factly. Matt was trying to act cool, but she was coming to know him well enough to realize he was anxious. His eyes skimmed the lobby as he spoke, and his movements, though quick, were somewhat erratic. His mood spread to Cathy, who felt she was on thorns.

At one minute to seven the clerk came and unlocked the door. The detective hurried forward and had a word with her.

"I wonder if Carr will have a gun," Cathy whispered.

"He doesn't usually, but Reilly has one. Let's hope he doesn't have to use it."

"Do we wait here?" she asked.

"We're only about five seconds away from the shop." His eyes kept moving from the front door in a circle around all possible approaches.

When a businessman entered the shop, Matt came to attention. "Carr might have an accessory," he said. "Maybe I should go into the shop...."

"The clerk was supposed to signal. What is the signal, by the way?"

"She taps her left ear—nonchalantly."

Cathy stood up and peered unconcernedly in the window. "He's only buying a newspaper," she reported. "No ear tapping going on."

Another man entered and bought a paper, then a woman bought something from the chocolate-bar-and-gum rack, also without ear tapping from the clerk. "I think I should go in," Matt said, worried.

"The clerk told me yesterday that the photo man came at seven. He should be here soon. Maybe Carr doesn't know he comes so early."

"Don't underestimate him." He jerked to attention, "Hey, who's that?"

A young man in a sort of casual uniform was approaching the shop. He wore a blue shirt and slacks. There was something inscribed on the pocket of his shirt. "That could be the man from the photo place," he said.

"He isn't carrying a package. He'd be carrying a bag or big envelope or something with the prints."

"I think I'll ask John to hang out in the shop. If I did it, Carr would recognize me." He hurried over and spoke to Reilly, who nodded and went into the little shop.

He came out not two seconds later, looking excited. "He's been robbed!" he exclaimed.

Matt leapt to his feet, frowning in confusion. "Who had? Carr?"

"No, the kid from Quick Developing. Some guy knocked him on the head in the parking garage and stole his bag of prints."

An angry oath exploded from Matt's lips, and he hurried into the shop with Cathy following behind him.

"Who did it? Did you get a good look at him?" Matt asked the delivery man. He was just a teenager really, and he looked stunned.

"Just a glance as I looked over my shoulder," the young man said. "He came at me from behind. A middle-aged guy with a cap and an ordinary jacket."

"A tweed jacket?" Cathy asked.

"No, it was a jeans jacket. He had on a baseball cap."

"It's got to be Carr," Matt said, suppressing the urge to howl and curse. "He's just changed his outfit since he knows I'm after him."

The youngster was rubbing the back of his head. "Did he hurt you much?" Cathy asked. "Maybe you should get that bump looked at."

"I'd better get back to the depot and report this. They'll probably call the police. Sorry, Ms. Ford," he said to the clerk. "It looks like you're going to have a lot of dissatisfied customers today."

"Yeah, even more than usual," she said fatalistically, but she didn't seem very concerned.

"I'd better check out the parking garage," Matt said. "Not that it'll do a bit of good. Carr will be long gone."

"Maybe somebody got a look at the car or license," Reilly suggested, and went with him.

Cathy stayed behind, talking with Ms. Ford. "What's this all about, anyway?" the clerk asked.

"Mr. Wilson had some important prints stolen," she said. Then she remembered that, in fact, what Jim Carr had stolen was a roll of unexposed film. The photo company probably just returned the role of negatives with a note. What would Carr make of that when he saw it?

Ms. Ford was looking at Cathy askance. "What kind of prints?" she asked suspiciously.

"Not that kind." Cathy laughed. "You have to take pictures like that to a discreet, private developer."

"Personally I wouldn't know," the clerk sniffed, and turned to serve a customer. Her disdainful look suggested that she didn't believe a word of it, and furthermore she wouldn't be a bit surprised if Cathy was the abandoned creature who had posed for the cheesecake shots.

Cathy wandered back to the lobby to wait for Matt. He was soon back with the house detective. "No luck," Matt said. "The parking garage was busy at this hour of the morning with service people arriving for work. Of the few people who noticed anything, no two saw the same thing. A small blue car, one man thought. Another said it looked brown to him, possibly a Mazda. Nobody got the license."

"At least Carr didn't get the pictures," Cathy said in an effort to cheer Matt up. He shot a repressive look at her.

Reilly looked first confused, then suspicious. "What do you mean, he didn't get them?" he demanded of Matt. "You said those prints were worth a million bucks. What have I been wasting my time on, anyway?"

"Of course he got them," Matt said. Cathy held her tongue, although she resented being made to look a fool. "Well, we've lost him. Since we're up so bright and early, we might as well have some breakfast. Will you join us, John?"

"I've got work to do," Reilly said in a rather surly way.

Matt and Cathy went to the coffee shop. "He obviously didn't buy your story," Cathy said. "Why didn't you tell him the truth?"

"I was afraid I wouldn't get his full cooperation to guard a set of blank prints. I just told him there was a picture of Carr on my film. It seemed easier."

"You might have told *me* what you'd told him. How was I supposed to know?"

"You weren't. It's my fault. *Mea culpa.* Sorry to inflict my bad mood on you. It's just my repeated failure to catch that wretch. He always escapes by the skin of his teeth. As you said, at least Carr didn't get the real photos, but he does make me feel like a prime jackass."

The waitress came with the coffeepot, and they ordered breakfast. "You're not the only one who feels stupid," Cathy said. "The clerk at the convenience shop thinks it was pornographic pictures of me that were stolen. I could tell by the look she gave me."

"Sorry again," he said, gazing at her as if he meant it. "Oh, what a tangled web we weave."

They sipped their coffee for a moment in thoughtful silence, then Cathy said, "Maybe you should have some copies of that picture of Carr made, some of those Wanted posters."

"He isn't officially wanted by the law—yet. Not unless I prove he's alive. Then the company can charge him with attempted fraud. Till then, I'm on my own, just counting on the goodwill of people like hotel detectives. And helpful cops," he added, his smile thanking her in particular.

He slid the picture of Carr out of his pocket to examine. His brow furrowed, and he took a closer look. "It's *fading!*" he exclaimed. "I don't believe this. I'm jinxed. Look, it's lighter, isn't it?"

He passed the picture over for Cathy to examine. It had faded somewhat, but not to the extent that the picture wasn't recognizable. "I'll check mine," she said, and drew it out of her purse. It was even worse.

"This happened to me once before when I had a friend develop film for me. My friend said he didn't leave the print in the fixative long enough," Matt said. "This is my fault, too. I kept trying to hurry Judge last night. By tomorrow there won't be a sign of Carr on these pieces of cardboard. My company will think I've become completely unhinged, sending them pieces of white cardboard marked urgent and confidential. I popped them in the mailbox when I left you last night."

"I don't know much about photo developing, but you said the fixative is used in developing the print. Maybe the negative is still all right."

Matt looked up hopefully. "You're right. I'm no expert, either, but that makes sense to me—unless he also botched the negative."

"Let's take the negative to a *real* developer and get it done over," Cathy suggested.

"And have Carr snatch it again? Damn the man's eyes. Now you see why I'm longing to catch him. He's made a fool of me a dozen times. Why would anyone that devious and sneaky and clever bother fudging an insurance policy? Why doesn't he just corner the market on pork bellies, or soybeans, or silver and make some real, semilegal money?"

"A million dollars seems pretty real to me, but you mentioned silver. He circled the ad for the Harbourfront Antique Market. Maybe he'll show up there, looking for old silver."

"Yes, in a black beard and mustache, or in a blond lady's wig and a skirt, or in a policeman's uniform, for all I know. He must read Sherlock Holmes."

Their breakfast arrived. After Matt had eaten his bacon and eggs, his confidence began to return. "That antique market—it's on Saturday, I think you said?"

"It's open every day, but on the weekend they have extra out-of-town agents. It's a bigger deal on the weekend."

Matt beat a tattoo on the tabletop with impatient fingertips. "He'll have checked out that envelope by now and know he isn't as clever as he thinks he is. I wonder what he'll do."

"Come back after me, I expect," Cathy said more calmly than she felt.

His fingers stopped tapping, his eyes flew to hers and his hand moved across the table to hold her fingers. "That's the most infuriating thing of all, involving you. Cathy, I think you should go home."

"You said it'd be hard to change my reservation."

"You may have to wait at the airport for a second flight. Someone's bound to cancel, sooner or later. In any case, there are trains, and buses—or you could hire a car."

It was a sensible suggestion, and while she appreciated that Matt wanted to protect her, she had not the slightest intention of obliging him. "I'm going to stick around. I want to see what happens."

"I'll let you know all about it. We'll be seeing each other again after this is over," he said persuasively. His tense expression softened to a smile. "You've been a great help, Cathy. I have every intention of keeping in touch with you."

She felt a sense of elation at both his words and his manner. If he was serious enough to mean it, she didn't plan to desert him. "I'm staying," she said simply.

"No, I really think you—"

"Hey, you don't own Toronto," she pointed out.

He accepted her decision with a pleasure that he couldn't quite conceal. Yet it was not an unalloyed pleasure. What if something happened to her? "At least move to another hotel. Register under an assumed name. And don't wear your red jacket. Maybe you could change your hair." He looked at her hair as he spoke. It was one of the first things he had noticed about her yesterday when he joined her for lunch. In this dim light it looked almost black. He liked the way it bounced when she moved her head. And last night, when he held her, it had felt like satin, all shiny and smooth. "But don't bleach it or anything," he added sternly.

"It's my hair. I'll bleach it if I want to," she retorted.

This drew a reluctant smile from him. "I see you don't like being told what to do. I'll make it a request, then. I wish you wouldn't bleach your hair. It's so nice the way it is."

This was more acceptable. In fact, it won him a rather shy smile. "I had no intention of bleaching it," she confessed.

"Good."

"Now, about Carr," she said, hastening back to business. While Cathy wanted to help, she wasn't eager to get herself killed. "I'll follow his trick and buy a hat. The hotel down at the harbor would be a convenient place for me to register, since we hope to follow Carr there tomorrow."

"I'll take over your room at the Plaza, just in case Mr. Carr comes calling again."

"Be sure you lock your door and put on the chain," she said, repeating his warning of the night before. "That's a request."

He studied her pensively, then said, "I don't mind being told what to do—by *you*. Why, you almost sound as though you care what happens to me, Cathy."

"Of course I care." His questioning expression eased into a smile. "I don't want to have to come back to Toronto and give evidence at your murder trial," she added. "It'd be a darned nuisance, and interrupt my work."

"So much for true love," he said with mock sorrow.

"What makes you an expert on true love?" she sniffed.

"I've—known a few women."

"Lived with them, you mean. Were they all 'true loves,' Matt?" she taunted.

"You make it sound as if my apartment has a revolving door! I only lived with one—" Her green eyes stared into his, and a flush warmed his cheeks. Why did he feel like a boy being chastised by the principal? What gave her the right to cross-examine him?

"When we first met, you implied you weren't living with anyone *at the moment*."

"It was the truth, though perhaps misleading. At most any moment, you'll find me living alone. Men do tend to vaunt their prowess to impress women."

"Men?" She gave a derisive laugh. "I thought only boys did that. I can assure you, only girls would be impressed by it. I'm not sure I'm doing justice to girls to say so," she added.

"Yes, I realized when you turned into a statue that you weren't impressed, and regretted my proud boast. I'm glad to have this chance to set the record straight."

The waitress returned with coffee, interrupting this promising line of conversation. Cathy wondered why he was telling her this. It seemed he was trying to improve her opinion of him. And it had worked, too. She wanted to hear more about the one he had lived with, but didn't want to reveal her rampant curiosity. Besides, whatever he said, it would only infuriate her. "What do you want to do today?" she asked.

Matt sensed her mood and wanted to patch up this pointless little quarrel. He wore a pensive, serious look when he replied, "I'd like to be alone with you, miles away from Jim Carr, but that's not what you meant, is it?"

That had sounded very much as if he meant it. "What should we be doing is what I meant," she replied.

"We could tour some antique stores, flash what remains of his picture and see if anyone recognizes him. I doubt he'd be so unwise, but he might have had a credit card issued under some alias. The company would have his address for sending the bills. We should do something about that negative, too. What you suggested, sending it to my company, is not a bad idea. Carr wouldn't hesitate to knock out a delivery boy, but I doubt he'd tackle the post office. He doesn't want the feds after him.''

"I have the negative with me. Let's do it right now,'' she said.

Matt thought about it a moment. "But then what if he gets you alone, and you don't have the picture and negative to give him? It might annoy him.''

"I'll give him this other film,'' she said, removing it from her purse. "The one we took yesterday at the art galleries.''

He thought about it a moment. "He doesn't know we got the other film developed, so that might do the trick.''

As soon as they had finished breakfast, they went up to Cathy's room and put the negative of Carr in an envelope, addressed to Matt's head office in Chicago. "I think the wisest thing to do is for me to check out of my room,'' Matt said. "We'll leave this room in your name, but I'll stay here—and pay for it, of course. Then we take you over to the Harbourfront Hotel.''

"Wouldn't it be better if I went alone, in case he's watching? I mean, we're not sure he knows we're working together.''

"He'll be busy for an hour or so, getting that film developed. If we leave now, it should be all right. And Cathy, I know it'll be a damned inconvenience to you, but could you leave at least some of your things in this room to give the appearance that you're still staying here?''

Cathy hastily considered her wardrobe, figuring out what she could leave behind. "I could take your suitcase and leave mine here, since he's already seen in it,'' she said. "And I have a few outfits from the tour that I won't need.''

"He won't know my toothbrush from yours," Matt added, "so if I just hide my razor and shaving cream... Maybe you could drape some lingerie over the shower rail. At a quick glance, that should convince him that you're still here."

"I need my underwear, Matt!" she objected.

"I suppose you do. Never mind, I'll buy some. What do you wear? Black lace?"

Black lace? Now where did he get that idea? "Carr doesn't know what I wear underneath, so it doesn't really matter."

"I'll get some of those wispy teddy things," he said with a bemused look.

She lifted a brow. "I don't wear those teddy things. They're uncomfortable. You must be thinking of someone else." She felt a burning anger and knew it was ridiculous. Matt's life hadn't begun the day he met her. He was a mature, sophisticated man who had probably had dozens of affairs.

He glinted a grin at her. "You've tried them at least, or you wouldn't know they're uncomfortable. You can't blame a guy for dreaming."

"Dream on," she said, and began gathering up what she would take with her.

Matt went to his room and returned with his packed suitcase. "We've run into a little problem with logistics here," he said. "Where can I keep my things? If you're ostensibly occupying this room, a man's suit and a pair of size-ten loafers might just give the show away."

"Oh, dear, it *is* becoming a tangled web, isn't it? I could take your suits in your suitcase to my room at the other hotel. I can see changing for dinner is going to involve taxis and things."

He gave a rueful grimace. "You'll look great in my business suit."

"I can't say you'll do much for my dress. I wear my gold hoop earrings with it. Shall I leave them behind for you?" she joked.

"You should never leave jewelry in your hotel room."

"That's what I tell all my robbery victims. Mine are costume jewelry, not real gold." Cathy realized her resentment was showing and determined to be less snippy.

"What we could do is just leave most of your things here, and you take most of my things with you, and we'll go to each other's room to change for dinner," he said.

"Right. Meanwhile, we should get a move on. Carr might be back soon. And since he might come to this room, I'll leave everything except what I vitally need and take most of your things."

She hastily tossed a few necessities in on top of Matt's belongings. While she was in the bathroom to gather up her toothbrush, she threw a brassiere over the towel rod, trying not to resent that Matt was so familiar with women's behavior. He wouldn't be very impressed with her lingerie if he favored black lace and teddies. Her bra wasn't black or lacy. It was white, and its only adornment was a little satin flower at the front.

They took a final look around the room before going downstairs for Matt to check out, looking all around the lobby as they passed through it. The doorman at the hotel hailed them a cab, and while they were driven to the other hotel, Cathy said, "I should pay you for the days I used my hotel room."

"Did you give them your credit card number?"

"Yes. I guess I'll have to sign it when you check out."

"And I'll have to repay you for the nights I use it. The hotel cashed a traveler's check for me. As soon as you're settled, we'll buy you that hat, then we'll go look at antique stores."

"Shouldn't you wear some disguise, too?"

"I doubt a hat will fool Carr, but we'll see what we can do."

Fortunately the tourist season hadn't reached the height yet, and the Harbourfront had a vacant room. Cathy signed in under her mother's maiden name, which made it impossible to use her credit card. Things were indeed becoming more complicated by the moment. She assumed Matt had cashed a very large check. He took some bills from his wallet and paid for the room for two days in cash.

He went up to the room with her while she settled in. The room was expensive, but it was luxurious, with a view of the harbor and two double beds. "We're going to need an accountant to straighten out our financial affairs when this is all over," Cathy said, sitting on the edge of one of the beds.

"Let me see, now I owe you for drinks last night—the one we did drink at the Alceze concert, and the one we didn't."

"That's on me. You paid for dinner," she pointed out.

"Yes, but dinner was a date. And anyway, I have an expense account. That concert was legitimate business. I'll owe you for the next couple of nights at the Plaza, since it'll be on your credit card."

"And you paid for this room, so I'll owe you for that."

"No, no. You're helping me, I'll pay for this room, too."

"No," she objected at once. Matt had noticed that independent streak in her before and liked it, but he was beginning to feel guilty. "I planned to stay in Toronto till Sunday. I want to pay for my own room," she insisted.

"But you're helping me!"

"You're paying for everything. All our meals and drinks and taxis and everything. Besides, you got stung a hundred bucks for that picture that's fading away."

"Why should you pay for that? I'm the one who wanted Carr's picture."

"That's true," she said.

"I'm putting you to the inconvenience of being hounded by Carr having your room searched. I should pay you for the inconvenience," he insisted. "If you'd at least let me pay, I wouldn't feel so guilty."

"Carr didn't take anything except a worthless photo stub. And you paid for everything yesterday. That hired car to take me to Etobicoke. I should pay for that. You only went because of me."

He saw there was no point arguing further with her. "This is going to take two years to straighten out. Let's go shopping. Hats first, then we go to the antique shops. There are some on Queen and some on Bloor, and probably ninety-nine others sprinkled all over the city."

"Since you first spotted him on Bloor, he might be living near there. Let's do the Bloor Street ones first."

"Good idea," he said with an admiring look. "You're an excellent colleague. How do you manage to keep your head when all about you are losing theirs?"

"My head's screwed on tight. Where would I put that new hat if I lost my head? Let's go shopping."

"You say that with all the enthusiasm of a surfer shouting 'Surf's up!'"

"So I like shopping," she admitted. "I'm not a shopaholic. I have it under control."

"Too bad," he murmured softly. "Don't you ever lose control, Cathy?"

"No, never." Then she added archly, "Well, as the guy in song said, 'hardly ever.' Come on."

They locked the door, looking all around for Carr as they went to the elevator, into the lobby and out onto the street. There was no sign of him, so they could relax for a while and enjoy themselves. Cathy intended to enjoy every minute of her time with Matt. And she meant to learn just what he meant by love, too.

Chapter Six

"Surprising how few hat stores there are nowadays," Matt said when they had traveled for several blocks along busy Yonge Street looking for one. "You'd think they had gone out of style or something." Yet as he glanced at the passing crowd, he noticed quite a few covered heads.

"Hat stores are out of style, but hats aren't. Lots of clothing stores we passed have hats in the window. They probably have a hat department. Let's try this one," she suggested when they came to a large department store.

The clerk at the cosmetics department just inside the door assured them they had both a ladies' and gentlemen's hat department, and headed them in the right direction.

"Ladies before gentlemen. We'll check the ladies' hats first," Matt said. Several counters holding all sorts of hats spread out around them. "Here's a nifty little number." He pointed to a black straw with a wide, soft brim that shadowed the eyes.

"With slacks and sneakers?" Cathy asked, staring at the elaborate concoction.

"Ah, a good point. But it would look marvelous on you." He lifted it from the featureless hat block and dropped it on her head. He cocked his own head aside and tilted the hat rakishly over her eye. "Very soigné," he said approvingly. "Not every lady could carry it off, but you can."

Cathy peered into the mirror. She looked like a different person—romantic, mysterious and glamorous. Was this the kind of woman Matt liked? Her mind kept harping back to that black lace teddy. She wasn't that kind of person. She was just a plain working girl.

"What do you think?" he urged.

"This is for eating watercress sandwiches under the spreading elms. I'm just a poor working girl." She removed the hat and returned it to the head stand.

Matt busied himself selecting other hats. "How about this one?" he said, offering her a different model. It was hardly a hat at all, but a large white silk rose with a wisp of lace attached to the front of it. He perched it on the back of her head and frowned.

Cathy adjusted it at the mirror, lowering the veil over her eyes. "I think it's worn like this," she said. It gave her a completely different look. She couldn't see very clearly through the veil, but the general impression was of a high-fashion model.

"Très chic," Matt said, "but it's crying out loud for a black dress and heels. Not your working uniform today." He saw the firm set of her jaw, and added hastily, "Or any other day. What was I thinking of?"

Cathy felt she was giving Matt the wrong impression, that she had no life beyond her job, no social activities. "Nice for a wedding or something, but since I'm wearing slacks and sneakers, maybe we'd better try something else," she said.

At the next counter she picked up a tightly woven natural straw hat with a simple black band. It was shaped like a man's fedora. She adjusted it in front of the mirror and liked the result. It had an air of understated fashion that didn't overwhelm the rest of her outfit. "I like this one," she said, turning her head to left and right.

She glanced up to see Matt's reaction. He was gazing at her in a bemused way. "It's you," he said. To himself he added, And so was black straw, and the white rose. Infinite woman. But why did she refuse to let that more beguiling female out of its shell? "Let's go with this one. How much—?"

"I'll get it," she said swiftly.

"It's part of your disguise. There's no reason you should pay for catching Carr. Let me pay. I want to."

"It's all right. I'll wear it after I get home." She glanced at the price tag. "It's not expensive, anyway. The black straw cost a fortune."

Matt swallowed the hot retort that rose to his lips. Why did she have to be so damned independent? It was unnatural. "If you insist."

"I do." She took it to the clerk and refused a bag. "I'll wear it, if you'll just cut off this price tag."

"Now it's my turn," Matt said, heading for the men's department. Again they encountered a bewildering array of hats. "And I said hats had gone out of style! Do you think a felt hat, or something more casual—a cap of some sort?"

After examining the wares, Cathy selected a tweed hat with a small, soft rim. When she turned around to show it to Matt, she found him posing in front of the mirror in a bowler. She would have laughed, except that he looked so darned good in it. It conferred an air of dignity and English reserve that he could carry off. He hastily removed the bowler and blushed. "I always wondered how I'd look in one of those. Just looking, don'tcha know? Jolly fine hat," he added in a caricature of a British accent.

"No excuses are needed. I'm not the saleslady. What do you think of this one?" She handed him her choice.

He set it on and examined it in the mirror. "I feel I should be carrying a meerschaum pipe and wearing spats."

"This isn't a deerstalker hat. It's for street wear."

He shook his head in distaste. "No, not my style."

She went in search of a different style. When she returned, he was posing in a white Stetson. "You have ten seconds to get that hat off, pardner," she warned, and laughed.

Matt refused to blush this time. "Don't you think it adds a certain *je ne sais quoi?*"

"Not without a horse and spurs. You'd stand out a mile. Here, try this one on."

It was an ordinary felt hat, but when Matt turned down the brim and turned it over his eye, he looked like a hood. He said out of the side of his mouth, "Now, see here, Lefty, I'm horning in on this town."

"Oh, dear. The cops would stop you and frisk you if you were seen in public in that. I think your windbreaker needs a cap, Matt, not a felt hat."

He reluctantly took off the felt hat and wandered to other counters, where he tried on a pith helmet and a top hat. "If you break into a soft-shoe shuffle, I'm leaving," Cathy warned. But again she thought he looked enchanting and debonair and very handsome. There was still a streak of the young boy in him, playing at dressing up in costumes. That surprised her in this sophisticated man. He looked good in any hat, and best of all, without one. His crisp black hair glimmered blue and amber under the lights, like a peacock's feathers. "Try this one on," she said, handing him a felt driving cap.

He dropped it insouciantly on his head. It was the least handsome of them all, but also the least likely to draw attention to him. "I feel like John Doe," he said glumly. "Is my economical four-cylinder car at the curb, ready to take me at a steady fifty miles an hour to my split-level in the suburbs, home to my wife and two-and-a-half children? Please tell me this is not me."

"It's not you, but that suburban man you're knocking is the backbone of America."

"I'm not knocking the *man*," he objected. "In case you didn't recognize him, that man was only a statistic. I'm knocking the hat. It makes me look anonymous. It robs me of my personality."

"That's what we want, isn't it?"

"I suppose so," he agreed with a last longing look at all the more interesting hats.

"You've been misrepresenting yourself, Matt. You're the one who likes shopping," she chided.

His sulky look strengthened the boyish impression. She found that attractive, too. "Only if I can buy what I want."

"Spoken like a true consumer. Ask not whether you have any use for the merchandise, but only whether you want it. Pay up, and let's get out of here. We're wasting time."

"That's not a very generous assessment of our shopping spree! I thought we were enjoying ourselves."

Cathy was surprised to see he was genuinely hurt. She admitted to herself that it had been fun and she had learned something about Matt, too. He wasn't so blasé that he didn't enjoy playacting. "Put on your hat like a good boy, and I'll buy you an ice-cream cone," she said, laughing.

"No, I'll buy you one. I'm getting off cheap. I should have paid for your hat," he said, and began walking off.

"I suggest you pay for your own, or you'll end up in the clink. And for heaven's sake, have the clerk cut the price tag off it. You look like a hick."

"See how you make me lose my head. If you'd bought the garden bonnet, I would have forgotten all about Carr."

"Did you really like it that much?" she asked.

He took her hand and squeezed it. "Maybe the model who was wearing it had something to do with it. I doubt I would have given it a second look by itself. Let's go."

"Go and pay for the hat, you mean."

He cleared his throat in embarrassment. "Of course, Lord, I'll be giving you the idea I'm a shoplifter, and you a cop! How much is it?" He took it off and glanced at the ticket. "Eighteen dollars! And I don't even like it."

"You could get a baseball cap for five bucks from a street vendor."

"Sorry, wrong ball club. I root for my home team."

He finally found a clerk and paid for the hat. "Now the fun begins. We hit the antique shops and flash Carr's picture," he said, "if there's anything left of it." He took out his picture and checked it. It was fading, but the print was still dark enough to recognize.

"How do we get to Bloor Street from here?" Cathy asked. "We could try the subway."

"Yes, and end up in the boonies, with your independence. We'll take a cab. I'm paying," he said firmly. "It's time to assert my masculine prerogative of paying the piper."

"So you can call the tune," she quipped.

"Is that what's behind your refusing to let me pay for anything?" he demanded sharply. "Just what tune do you think I have in mind? Good Lord, I'm not that crude!"

She saw that he was really offended, and wanted to make things right between them. Was that why she insisted on paying her own way? She admitted that Matt hadn't tried to take advantage of her. Maybe it was time to relax her guard a little. "Sorry if I unwittingly stepped on your toes," she said.

He settled down when she apologized. "In case you haven't noticed," he said apologetically, "I'm only wearing running shoes. Soft toes."

He hailed a taxi and asked the driver about antique shops that specialized in silver. The driver said Bloor Street was as good a place as any and took them there. The remainder of the morning was largely a waste of time, but an enjoyable waste of time. They walked and argued and laughed like old friends. They toured five shops, flashing the picture of Carr, but as the picture was so unclear and growing dimmer by the moment, no one could identify him positively.

"A man, about fifty years old, medium build, snuff-colored hair, a cycle-shaped scar on his right thumb, likes old silver," Matt said at each shop.

"Would you mean Mr. MacIver from Rosedale?" one clerk asked. "He's been coming in once a month for ten years. I never noticed a scar, though. I sold him a dandy set of George III salt cellars last month for his collection. I'm always glad to see him buy things, since he has willed his collection to the museum."

"No, this would be a newish customer. Say, within the last few weeks."

"I get a lot of people in looking. I don't remember selling a piece to anyone fitting that description."

The story was similar in each shop. In the last one a sharp-eyed female clerk looked at them with interest. "I do remember seeing that scar. When was it? Last week, I think. He didn't buy anything, but he was interested in a Victorian tea set. It wasn't the price he objected to. He was a tourist, you see, and he was traveling about, so he thought the tea set would be hard to carry. I told him I could mail it to his home, but he didn't seem interested in that."

This certainly sounded like Carr. He didn't have a set address, and sending it to his wife's home might arouse curiosity, as it was watched intermittently. "Did he mention where he was staying in town?" Matt asked.

She thought a minute. "No, I don't think so, but it would be a hotel, wouldn't it? At least he didn't mention knowing anyone in town. He was quite knowledgeable about old silver. I very nearly sold him a small pedestal rose bowl, seventeenth-century English, but he noticed a little dent in the bottom rim. He only collects perfect pieces. He could have had it repaired, but he was afraid the repair would show."

"Did he say he'd be back?" Matt asked eagerly.

She shook her head. "No, he didn't. He asked about other local shops. I told him about the Harbourfront Antique Market. There are a dozen silver dealers there. Have you tried Harbourfront?"

"No, but we will. Thank you," Matt said, and they left the shop. "Well, we know he was here, but that doesn't do us much good, does it?"

"Harbourfront is open all week. We could try it today," Cathy suggested.

"Let's have some lunch first. I'm tired and hot and hungry. It's hard work, pounding the pavements. We'll see if we can find a Chinese restaurant for you."

They walked along, checking all the restaurants, but couldn't find one specializing in Chinese cuisine in this district. "I'd settle for a hamburger," Cathy said. She was more tired than hungry and just wanted to sit down and rest.

"We can do better than that. How about the Plaza, for old time's sake? It's our first anniversary. Twenty-four hours ago we first met there, and I more or less pinched your camera."

"So you did stand in front of it on purpose! I thought so."

"Suspicious woman." He peered down at her. "You were supposed to say 'Has it only been twenty-four hours? I feel as if I've known you forever.' Where's your sense of romance?''

"You read too many Victorian novels."

"How did you guess?" he smiled, and tucked her hand under his elbow. "Actually the Plaza will probably be filled up by now. It was yesterday."

"We could nip in and see if Carr's hanging around. I'll go, just in case he doesn't know we're working together."

"He knows by now."

"It'll bolster the idea that I'm still staying at this hotel," she added.

"That's a good point. We'll give it a try."

They went to the Plaza, but couldn't get a table and didn't see any sign of Carr. Matt had a word with the house detective, but Carr hadn't been spotted. "I doubt if he'll come back here after knocking out the Quick Developing delivery man," Reilly said.

"Nobody saw him."

"He can't be sure of that."

They went across the road to another hotel and discussed the case while they had lunch. "He's probably skipped town by now," Cathy said.

"Not while he knows we have that film with his picture on it. He's here, waiting his chance."

"He has a lot of nerve if he is."

"He's not short of nerve, or brains," Matt admitted. "I imagine he's changed his appearance. He's probably wearing a mustache and beard—or even a dress."

"Not with a mustache and beard, I hope."

"You know what I mean. He'll be well disguised."

"He might use a cane or crutches, or something to distract interest from his face. Criminals do that sometimes," Cathy said.

She began examining the clients of the dining room, looking for beards or mustaches or other concealing touches. "There's a man in a black beard just sitting down behind you, but he's speaking with a German accent," she whispered to Matt.

"That sounds like something he'd pull," Matt said excitedly. "Is he alone?"

"No, he's with a woman. She doesn't have any accent."

The man turned to look for a waiter, and Cathy got a good look at his face. He looked nothing like Carr. "False alarm," she said.

No one else in the restaurant bore any trace of Carr or anything that might be used as a disguise. Over a simmering bowl of bouillabaisse, Matt asked, "What made you decide to become a cop, Cathy? I know your dad is one, but your mom's a nurse. You didn't become a nurse."

"Are you implying that nurses are care givers, nurturers, whereas policemen are enforcers, authoritarian figures?" she parried.

He looked aghast. "It was just an innocent question! Don't read a whole attitude problem into it. I'm just curious about you. I wish you wouldn't be so touchy."

She had done it again, gone shooting off at the lip without stopping to think. "I am touchy on that point," she admitted. "Actually I'm squeamish. I'm scared at the sight of blood."

"You!" he exclaimed. After the shock wore off, he found it rather endearing that she had this weakness.

"You sound surprised that I have any feelings."

"No, that you have a weakness. You seem so cool, so in charge."

Cathy had never thought of herself in that light. If she seemed cool, it was only an effort to hide her insecurities. She still felt some need to do so. "I don't faint at the sight of blood or anything, but I wouldn't want to have to deal with it on a regular basis. Dad always seemed happy with his work. It's varied and interesting and useful, so I gave it a shot. And I like it."

Matt listened attentively, encouraging her to expand on her work with questions. "I bet you're good at it," he said when she stopped.

"How did you come to be an insurance investigator?" she asked.

"I knew I didn't want to sit behind a desk all my life. I like the variety and adventure of my work."

As he expanded on some of his cases that had taken him to Nice and Rome, it all sounded glamorous and exciting to Cathy. It reinforced the impression she had of him as a sort of international playboy. It would be foolish to think anything permanent would come of this chance meeting.

They had a leisurely lunch, and as they lingered over coffee, Cathy said, "Do you want to head downtown to check out more antique shops this afternoon?"

"It seems a waste of time. Even if he bought anything, he would probably have paid cash and not left an address. He's very cautious. I've about run out of ideas." His shoulders slumped, and his expression bordered on defeat.

In an effort to cheer him up, Cathy said, "We could go to Harbourfront's antique area. A couple of the antique dealers suggested it. And we can buy a newspaper to see if there are any other clubs featuring classical guitar. For tonight, I mean. I don't imagine he'd risk going back to Serge Alceze."

Matt gave her a rueful smile. "I'm ruining your holiday. You probably wanted to look up old friends or go to galleries or shopping or something." He had been a selfish beast, using up her vacation time on his problem.

"I don't have any old friends here. I've been to one gallery, which is more than I'd normally go to. I've been shopping and seen some of the sights. My big plans are just to hang out, maybe take a bus tour, eat and drink and generally goof off. I'm having a great time—really." Cathy realized that she wasn't just saying it to appease him. She really was enjoying herself and she didn't bother to fool herself as to why. It was Matt's company she enjoyed.

"Let's take a guided bus tour," he suggested. The least he could do was spend half a day doing something she enjoyed.

Cathy took the idea he was just trying to make up to her for monopolizing her time. "I'd rather go to the antique market," she said, and meant it. "He might be there, Matt. We can take a tour anytime. You have to strike while the iron's hot. Carr was in town this morning. Now, let's get cracking before he leaves."

"You're sure you don't mind? I can do it alone, if you want to—" He held his breath, hoping she wouldn't change her mind. He had always preferred to work alone before. A partner just slowed him down, but he had to admit that Cathy was just as determined as he was and at least as knowledgeable.

"I don't."

"Don't what?"

"Don't want to do whatever you were going to say. I want to find Carr. I have a grudge against him, too, you know. He broke into my hotel room and stole the film that was in my name. Who does he think he is, stealing my blank film?"

"Well, if you're sure." He looked at her from over the rim of his coffee cup. He felt he could drown in those crystal-clear eyes. "You're being a great sport about this, Cathy."

She felt guilty, accepting praise for doing what she wanted to do. Or did the guilt have a different origin? Was it because she was trying to hide from Matt the reason she insisted on helping him was that she wanted to be with him? What they were doing wasn't as important as the fact that they were doing it together. "I was taught that helping catch crooks is everyone's job."

"I'm just working for my company, not for the good of mankind," he pointed out.

"You're chasing a crook—the same difference."

"Hmm." His brows drew together in a frown.

"What's the matter?"

"I was hoping your stubbornness had a more personal reason—like you enjoyed being with me, maybe?" His tone made it a question, and her innate honesty caused a blush to lighten her cheeks.

"It doesn't detract from my stubbornness—determination—that you're a fairly personable male." His frown eased, and his expression assumed a satisfied air. "I'm not stubborn," she added.

He weighed her mild compliment. "A fairly personable male. Well, it's better than being a jerk, I suppose." An impish grin tugged at his lips. "And may I say I enjoy working with a fairly personable female, too?" Before she could respond, he lifted his hand and beckoned the waiter for the bill. The waiter took Matt's credit card and left.

"You should show him Carr's picture and ask if he's ever been here," Cathy suggested. She would not satisfy him by commenting on that "fairly personable female." That was just his petty revenge for her description of him.

"A good idea. I wonder why I didn't think of it, since you're not outstandingly beautiful. I'm seldom distracted by a merely personable female."

His tone, and that smile, belied his words. It was possible to read into his speech that he did find her outstandingly beautiful, and she had to fight to hold in a smile.

He showed the waiter the picture, but it was fading so quickly that the waiter just shrugged. "I haven't seen any ghosts around lately."

"We can forget this piece of cardboard," Matt said as they left the hotel. "It's no longer of any use."

She pulled her copy out and looked at it. "Mine's no better. Never mind, Matt. We've both seen Carr. We'll recognize him if he's at the antique market. Let's go."

"Is that where we're going?"

"Yes," she said, since Matt seemed to have lost his rudder.

The taxi dropped them at the quay. They stood a moment, admiring the sailboats on the sparkling water. "Since he likes sailing, maybe he keeps a boat here," she said.

"He doesn't really like sailing. He just took it up to arrange the accident, but it's something to check if our other leads peter out."

They entered the mall and began looking for Carr at the stalls and shops featuring old silver. Cathy enjoyed browsing through the shelves of beautiful silverware, imagining the tables they had graced, and that obsolete life-style, with maids to clean the silver. They didn't see Carr, but Matt posed his question at each stop and got a few nibbles. Without a picture no one could be certain, but a woman at one stall and a man at another thought he sounded familiar.

"If he was a regular customer, you'd think someone would remember him more clearly," Cathy said, frowning.

"I imagine he makes it a point to be as unnoticeable as he can. He wouldn't do a lot of talking about himself."

They lingered around the mall for an hour in all, and when they came out, a few artists and artisans had set up stalls on the street. The glowing sun was cooled by a breeze from the lake, making it a pleasant spot for a walk. One woman was doing quick charcoal sketches of customers. Her floppy hat and longish skirt reminded Cathy of a hippie. She was working on a little girl, who was unhappy to have to sit still for twenty minutes.

"Just a little longer, Megan," her mother said. "It's a surprise for Daddy's birthday. Don't you want to surprise Daddy?"

"I want to go home, Mommy."

While the child and mother argued, Matt asked Cathy, "Why don't we get a sketch of you?"

"I don't want a sketch of me. I have a mirror."

"So have I, but my mirror won't show me you when we're apart."

"You'll have that picture you took yesterday at the Eaton Center," she reminded him.

"A sketch is more personal. This woman's really quite good," Matt said, looking at a number of sketches she had tacked up on her stall.

The woman, sensing a sale, said over her shoulder, "I'll be finished in five minutes, if you can wait. Those are some sketches I did on spec. They didn't sell, obviously. I put them up to let potential customers see samples of my work."

Matt examined them, and since he didn't seem interested in leaving, Cathy joined him. The sketches featured interesting characters: an old lady with a rugged, lined face; a young man, wearing a punk cut known as a Mohawk—with a wedge of hair down the center of his head—a Yuppie man in an oxford shirt. They both saw the sketch of Carr at the same time. They exchanged a startled look and turned to the artist. She was just accepting payment from the mother. When her client left, Matt asked, "When did you do this?" and handed her the sketch of Carr.

"I usually only come here on the weekend. I did that last Sunday afternoon. Why, do you know him?"

"Yes. How come he didn't take it with him?" It seemed incredible to Matt that Carr would leave evidence like this sitting around to incriminate him.

"He didn't even know I did it. He was just standing, gazing out at the water. I thought he had an interesting face—sort of medieval, you know, the way the eyes are sunk into his face and the features all close together.''

"Do you know his name?''

"I didn't get to speak to him. I hoped he'd stroll this way and I'd show it to him. But then I got a different customer and I didn't see him leave. Maybe he'll buy it this weekend. I've seen him around a few times.''

Matt and Cathy exchanged a delighted look. "Oh, really?'' Matt said. "I'd like to buy it to—to surprise him.'' He flashed a winning smile. "Is it for sale?''

"It isn't finished. You'll notice I just started the neck and shoulders.''

"That's all right. Jim won't mind. How much?''

"Twenty-five dollars,'' she said, looking at him with a question in her eyes. "Say, is there something funny about this guy?''

"Why do you ask?'' Matt countered.

"I thought he was acting kind of strange. Looking over his shoulder, you know, as if—I don't know. I just remember that every time I looked at him to check a feature, he moved his head. The sketch isn't very good, I'm afraid.''

"Oh, I think it's very good. It's excellent. I'll take it. And do you have a business card, in case I want to get in touch with you again?'' Cathy figured he might want the woman as a witness.

"Right here,'' she said, and handed him one from the stack she kept beside her. "Do you want your sketch taken, miss?'' she asked Cathy.

"We have to go now,'' Cathy said. "Maybe another time.''

Matt handed the artist the money, rolled up the sketch and they left.

"I hope he comes on Saturday. I have to leave Sunday,'' Cathy said. "Wouldn't that be just my luck.''

"I have no argument with lady luck at the moment," Matt said, biting back a big grin. "We've earned a reward. What would you like to do?"

"I wish you could stay until Sunday," she said. "But you said yourself it'll be hard to get a seat on the plane. They're booked up pretty solid in the summer tourist season."

"We'll charter one!" he said rashly. "If we don't catch him Saturday, the company can foot my bill and fly me back."

"That'd cost a fortune!"

"My company will save a million if we get him. They're not likely to balk at chartering a plane. Even if I miss him this time, I have a witness now who's seen him alive, when he's supposed to be dead. It's enough to hold up the payment a few more months. Now, back to my question. What would you like to do with the rest of this afternoon?"

"Keep looking. There's no guarantee he'll be at the antique fair on Saturday."

"Time to stop and smell the flowers," he said. "I suggest we take a break, do a guided bus tour. We can look for Carr from the window, if your conscience bothers you. No reason why it should. This is really my job. But hit and miss is the best we can do till tomorrow. We can do that just as well from a bus as anywhere else."

She knew he was doing it for her, and as she couldn't think of anything more useful to do, she agreed. Of course they didn't spot Carr during their tour of Toronto, but they saw the sights of the city and talked with fewer arguments than before. Cathy found it possible to let her guard down a little with him. She noticed that he didn't rush in to take advantage of it, unless holding her hand could be called taking advantage.

Chapter Seven

"We'll get all gussied up and go out for dinner," Matt said as they dismounted from the sight-seeing bus. "I'll find out at the Plaza which is the best Chinese restaurant."

"The Lichee Gardens is famous. We should make reservations on a Friday night. Now, where should we go first?"

"The Plaza's closer. We'll go there to let you change."

"I have my makeup at the Harbourfront Hotel," she said.

"Then you can put on your face when we go there for me to change." He took her hand and ran to catch a taxi. "We should think about living together. It would make things a lot simpler," he said nonchalantly as he opened the taxi door. Cathy, preceding him into the cab, didn't see the tense expression he wore.

Living together was a big step, and although Matt spoke casually, he had been giving the matter a lot of thought. He liked Cathy very much and wanted to get to know her better. Once this visit was over, they'd be living in different cities, and he really wanted to go on seeing her.

His casual tone made it sound like a joke, but Cathy considered it a joke in bad taste. "Live together, when we've only known each other for one day?" she said, settling herself into the cab. "That's sort of radical, isn't it? And where would you suggest?" she continued, speaking ironically. "Somewhere halfway between Chicago and Schenectady? That would be about Pittsburgh, wouldn't it?"

Matt gave the driver their destination. She thought that was the end of the other conversation, but when he had settled in, he said, "I kind of like Cleveland." He spoke facetiously to hide his hurt.

"Neither Pittsburgh nor Cleveland is exactly handy to our hotels."

The cab left the curb with a squeal of tires, throwing Cathy against Matt. He put an arm around her shoulder protectively, and said, "All I said was, maybe we should think about it. Something for the future. No harm in exploring possibilities, is there?"

"It doesn't take much exploration to realize Cleveland's a little far for me to commute to my office."

Matt noticed her lack of enthusiasm, and while he wasn't exactly surprised, he had expected some show of interest. "Hmm. One of us would have to change jobs, then. My company doesn't have an office in Schenectady."

She gave a careless shrug. "Then that's that."

"Not necessarily. You work for the police. They have plenty of cops in Chicago."

Suddenly he didn't sound so casual. There was real interest in the dark gray eyes gazing at her. "Yes, and even more in New York," she added irrelevantly. Her mind was reeling when she realized he was serious.

"What's New York got to do with it?"

"What's Chicago got to do with it, for that matter? I work in Schenectady. I'd hardly move to Chicago just to make it easier to change for dinner—even with you." She added the last phrase with a joking smile and a pat on his arm.

His fingers closed over hers and squeezed. He inclined his head close to hers, and said in a warm voice, "People who live together do other things besides have dinner."

There was no mistaking his meaning. Cathy felt a rising urge to give him a piece of her mind, but since he probably meant no harm—in fact he probably thought he was flattering her—she decided to end this conversation. "Does Carr like Chinese food?" she asked.

Matt frowned at her trick, but answered the question. "He prefers Italian. That's why I've been urging it on you."

"Maybe we should go to an Italian restaurant this evening, then."

"There must be dozens—probably hundreds—in the city. The odds of hitting the one Carr is at are pretty slim. I vote for Chinese. I wonder if they have good Chinese restaurants in Cleveland?" he added with a mischievous grin. "I noticed how adroitly you changed the subject."

"It seemed a fairly pointless conversation, since neither of us has any intention of moving to either Cleveland or Pittsburgh."

The taxi pulled in at the hotel, and they went up to room 617. Cathy kept harking back in her mind to that suggestion that they should live together. She noticed Matt hadn't used the word "marriage." She could easily enough get transferred to Chicago. In fact, she'd been thinking it was time to transfer to a larger city, but she had no intention of doing it just to live with him. In fact, she wasn't flattered that he'd suggested it.

Matt had obviously forgotten the conversation altogether. He chattered on about other things. "Since it's early, we could have a drink sent up to our room and just relax for a while," he said.

Cathy pulled herself back to attention. "I'd like to have a shower before I change."

"So would I." She sensed some undercurrent in his voice and looked at him in alarm. But he continued blandly, "This having two rooms presents logistical problems that could easily be avoided if—"

Before he could say more, Cathy interrupted him. "You're the kind of man who sees the problems. I see the solution. You have a drink here while I shower and change, then I'll have one at the other hotel while you shower and change."

"Drinking alone is bad for you." He unlocked the door and gave her a heavy mock-frown. "I have the feeling your heart isn't in this living-together-in-Cleveland idea. Which is it you object to, Cleveland or me?"

"I have nothing against Cleveland." She smiled demurely.

He opened the door and stopped in his tracks. "Good Lord! We've been hit by a hurricane!"

Peering over his shoulder, Cathy saw the room was in chaos. The bed had been pulled apart, the mattress half on the floor. The drawers of the desk had been pulled out and turned upside down, leaving a welter of leaflets and stationery in its wake. "Hurricane Jim Carr," she said in a hollow voice.

As they entered the room, she felt a rising tide of frustration and anger at the devastation. Her personal belongings were tossed helter-skelter around the room, the bed and dresser. She picked up her red jacket. He had pulled off the top pocket, leaving a rent down to the hem. It was completely destroyed.

Matt's face was palely grim as he looked around the room. "I didn't realize Carr has such a violent temper. Until now he's been very cool. We've got him worried—it seems he doesn't react well to stress." He turned to Cathy. "We've got to get you out of here, fast. I'll see about flying you home."

"I'm not leaving," she said firmly. "Look what he did to my best jacket." She held it up for him to examine.

His lips clenched at Carr's stunt. "At least it's only a jacket. Thank God you weren't in it at the time. I'll call the airport." He went toward the phone.

"I wouldn't leave without catching him now, not for a million dollars," she said, chin up, eyes shooting green sparks. "This time he's gone too far. Foraging through my suitcase was bad enough—stealing the film and hitting that poor delivery boy was worse, but this time he's really done it. We're going to catch this jerk, Matt."

"*I'll* catch him. It's my job. I never should have dragged you into this in the first place." His voice was tense with worry. What had he been thinking of, drawing an innocent young woman into his problems? If he'd had any idea Carr was so violent—

"I'm in now," she announced, "and I'm in until we catch him."

Matt looked at her helplessly. He had never seen such a determined expression in his life. She wasn't going to give in, and he was equally determined to keep Cathy out of it from now on. It was bad enough to involve any outside party, but Cathy was becoming especially dear to him.

While they stood, eyes locked in a silent battle, there was a tap at the door, and Mr. Reilly stepped in. He stopped and gaped at the room. "What on earth happened?"

"Carr got in," Matt said curtly.

"I was on the lookout for him, but there was an emergency on the third floor. Some lady phoned that a man was trying to break in. Turned out it was a couple of kids looking for their parents' room. I'll call the desk and arrange to have a man on this full-time." Cathy picked up her belongings while Reilly placed the call. He hung up. "All set. I'll stay here, and a replacement will take over downstairs. Sorry about this."

"We'll be in touch," Matt said. Cathy packed her belongings and they went downstairs to take a taxi to the Harbourfront Hotel. They were quiet as they drove through the traffic. Matt was trying to figure out a way to keep Cathy from further reprisals by Carr, and Cathy was wondering what they could safely do to catch him. The attack on her room had escalated the mood to real danger. And that meant it was time to call in the police.

As soon as they were in her room, Cathy said, "It's time to call the police in on this, Matt. You said he'd never been formally charged with a crime. We've got him on breaking and entering now, as well as malicious destruction of property."

This was the speech he had been dreading from the moment he met her. He had to squelch that idea fast. "No way," he exclaimed angrily. "The police will only scare him off."

"They're not a bunch of flat-footed Keystone cops, you know," she shot back. "They won't send in a bunch of uniformed officers."

"Carr can smell a cop a mile away. They'd be of no use, anyway. They go about their dull, plodding way, filling in reports and eventually putting out an APB after the suspect is long gone."

This comprehensive slur on her and her father's whole career set her heart pounding. Her lips turned white in fury. "Are you calling me a dull plodder?"

"I didn't say you! You take everything too personally."

"It's pretty hard not to. You forget, I'm a cop."

"Not for one minute," he retorted hotly. "I should never have let you join me. I knew you'd want to drag in the police. Cops are all alike. Hidebound authoritarians following interminable procedures, messing up my months of work.''

Every word he said pushed her deeper into anger. ''I didn't try to take over—unfortunately. You could have caught him last night in my room if you'd done as I suggested. No, you had to go to a concert—watch Alceze fiddle while Rome burned.''

That jibe struck a nerve. ''I can't be everywhere at once. Unlike the police, I don't have an army to back me up. I depend on instinct and ingenuity. I work alone and I move fast.''

''If you can call eight month's surveillance without an arrest 'fast.' Sorry I don't have your ingenious instinct for messing up. I'm just a dull, plodding cop.''

The truth of her accusation cut his pride to the quick. ''If the shoe fits...'' he retaliated without thinking.

It was the last straw. ''You like to work alone, so I guess you want me to butt out.'' Cathy marched to the door and flung it wide. ''Goodbye, Matt, and good luck. It looks like you're going to need it.''

Matt realized he had gone too far and already regretted it. He glanced from Cathy to the door. ''I don't want you to butt out,'' he said. ''I got carried away. I didn't mean it.''

''So you don't mind if I report this break-in.'' She watched as his expression stiffened to opposition.

''I'd prefer you didn't. Can't you trust me?''

Sure, she could trust him to turn on her and insult her after all her help. ''I go by the book. Sorry.'' Her voice was hard, to quell the rising quaver of regret.

Matt's jaw clenched. He didn't trust himself to speak. He just stormed out of the room. Cathy slammed the door behind him. Her hands were trembling, but she didn't notice. She was too busy reviewing all his insults. It was another five minutes before she began to think of her own part in the argument. She knew she had wounded his pride by taunting him about not catching Carr. Was that why she had said it, to retaliate? She had let her temper run free, and it wasn't just because he wouldn't call the police, either. It was the way he talked idly about love, which only meant he wanted a woman "at the moment."

Matt went down to the lobby, telling himself he was glad to be on his own and trying to assess the damage the police would do to his case. He had tried working with them in Atlantic City. It had been a disaster. But Cathy had helped a lot. If he'd listened to her last night, he'd have Carr in custody now. But that wasn't why he stopped and turned around.

Cathy heard a tap at the door. When she answered, Matt said, "I'm sorry. The police might want to talk to me, as well." It was his pretext, to save face.

"I didn't call them." They exchanged a questioning smile. "Hey, it's only a torn jacket," she said, but her smile said the rest. She was deviating from the book—for him.

"Does this mean I have my helper back?"

"If you think I won't slow you down too much," she said, but with a smile.

"I must have sounded like an idiot."

"Yeah, must be that ingenious flair you mentioned. I'm going to take that shower now." She took her suitcase and went into the bathroom, smiling.

Matt made the dinner reservation and called for the drinks. Then he tried to devise a plan to keep Cathy out of further danger. She already knew about the antique show tomorrow. There wasn't a good-enough excuse in the world to keep her away. She was one determined lady. If he left her behind tomorrow, Carr might come after her while she was alone. Or equally bad, she'd go to the market on her own. Maybe she'd be safer with him. He'd hold on to her hand tightly, and if he spotted Carr, he'd find some excuse to nip off after him alone, leaving Cathy safely behind.

It wasn't much of a plan, but it was the best he could come up with. When the drinks arrived, he sat sipping his beer and thinking about Cathy Auden. His attraction for her was getting out of hand.

It seemed only minutes later that she joined him, but his watch told him she'd been gone half an hour. She looked freshly minted, with her dark hair shining and her skin glowing from the shower. She had changed into a deep blue dress that lent a darker hue to her eyes. The dress hugged her curvaceous body, lending her an air of sophistication.

His eyes moved slowly from hair to face to body, then back up. When he spoke, his voice was husky. "You look marvelous." He moved across the room, bringing her her drink. Their eyes held in a long gaze as they clinked glasses.

The air suddenly felt close, and to establish a less-charged atmosphere, she said, "Did you get the reservation?"

"For eight. No hurry." His eyes didn't waver from hers.

She was reluctant to break the mood when he was looking at her as if he wanted to kiss her. She moved her eyes, because the message they were receiving made her very nervous. "It's after seven. You'd better have your shower, Matt."

"They won't give away our table if we're a minute late."

"I think I'll run down and get a newspaper to read while you shower." This made an excuse to move away.

His hand came out and caught hers. "I don't want you out of my sight." His warm fingers felt like a caress.

"In other words, you want me here to protect you."

"I definitely want you here." Was it that husky voice or the dark gray eyes that said so much more than his words? Matt reached for the phone, still holding on to her hand. "Would you send today's newspaper up to room 710 right away, please?" He put down the phone. "The paper'll be right up. I'll be in the next room, having my shower. I want you to look out the peephole before you open the door to take the newspaper. Promise?''

"And if Mr. Carr has insinuated himself into a job at the hotel and happened to overhear that we ordered a paper, and is carrying it with a gun concealed underneath, what should I do, Matt?'' she asked, biting back a grin.

He drew his lips into a line and glared. "Give him a small tip—more financial complications for our accountant—but don't invite Carr in for drinks.''

"I'll just Mace him in the hallway and call you.''

"Mace? Isn't that illegal? And you a member of the police force.'' He made a *tsk*ing sound.

"Yes, it is, but Mom had a can before it was illegal, and she gave it to me when I left home. My superior officer doesn't know.''

"I won't tell him he's harboring a depraved lawbreaker on his staff. You're corrupting my rigid morals,'' he added with a teasing grin. Then he lifted her hand and placed a quick kiss in the palm before releasing it.

He left to take his shower. Cathy closed her fingers as if to hold in that kiss. She took her drink to the window and gazed down at the waterfront without seeing it. Matt might be a playboy, but he was a charming one. Her heart twisted at the memory of that kiss, so old-fashioned and romantic. Did he suit his attack to his prey? He had some idea by now that she wasn't exactly a swinger.

What was the point of these romantic repinings? She shook away the wisps of regret and thought about business. She didn't think Carr could know they were here. He wouldn't have hung around the Plaza after ripping up her room. But when the tap came at the door, the voice announcing "room service" sounded suspicious to her. A little shiver scuttled up her spine. She peered through the hole at a perfectly innocent young man with blond hair. She opened the door and gave him a tip, as Matt had suggested.

She took the paper to the desk and opened it at the entertainment section to see if she could find any amusement likely to appeal to Carr. The only classical guitarist in town was Serge Alceze. She agreed with Matt that Carr wouldn't likely show up there a second time, but they'd drop around, just in case. Carr certainly had enough nerve for anything, so they couldn't just rule it out. There were plenty of other musical shows on in town. She didn't think a man of Carr's age would go to a rock concert or to any of the clubs featuring rock music, though.

The Imperial Room at the Royal York was advertising a band from the swing era. The ad mentioned dancing, which would require a date. Was Carr seeing other ladies during this long absence from his wife? She got her pen out and marked the ad to mention to Matt.

It was forty-five minutes before he emerged from the bathroom, smelling of some spicy lotion and with his hair slicked down. "What took you so long?" she asked.

"Ah, you missed me. That's a promising sign. We men, being such virile, lusty creatures, have to shave."

"It can't take forty-five minutes."

"I do my best thinking under the shower."

"That's not very handy, is it? In an emergency, I mean, to have to scoot around till you find a shower."

"Luckily one was handy in this emergency. I had a lot of thinking to do." His bemused smile suggested that he'd been thinking about her, not Carr.

"Are you going to finish your drink?"

He flicked a quick glance at it. "It's gone flat. Some things do, after a while," he added thoughtfully. "It's the bubbles I like."

"Do you also buy steak for the sizzle? The drink's still good. All that's gone is the carbon dioxide."

Matt frowned over what they'd been saying. Was that what was wrong in his relationships? All bubbles and sizzle

and no real substance? It would be nice to have a deeper relationship with a woman. Someone to share your problems, as well as your triumphs and apartment. That first fine
flurry of romance couldn't last when you were living with
someone. Maybe that was where he'd made his mistake,
trying to drag it out instead of letting it grow into something more solid and enduring—like love.

"Are you still with me, or have you gone into a trance?"
Cathy asked. "If you're not going to drink it, let's go. It
might take a while to find a taxi at this hour."

He gave her a strange look. "I'll try it. Who knows,
maybe I'll like it." He lifted the glass and finished it. "I
prefer it with bubbles," he said, "but I think I could get
used to it like this."

"You should have put the cap back on. That holds the
bubbles in longer."

"What a wise lady you are. Of course I should have put
the cap back on. You have to look after a drink if you don't
want it to go flat. I always put the cap back on the tooth-
paste. Do you?"

"I seem to have missed a beat in this conversation, but
yes, I do. I don't like messy bathrooms."

"Oh, good. Neither do I. Excuse me." He rushed into the
bathroom and picked up the towels. Cathy had left the
bathroom as neat as a pin for him. He hadn't been a perfect roommate himself, now that he thought about it. He'd
been living alone too long, with a maid coming in to pick up
after him. Maybe he hadn't been putting enough into his
relationships. He didn't like panty hose and lingerie on the
shower curtain rod, but no doubt his friend hadn't much
cared for towels in the tub, either. It took two caring people
to make love work. You couldn't be careless about the finer
points of polite behavior.

In fact, you had to be more careful when you were in close
daily contact with someone. The Japanese had taught

themselves that, hadn't they? Millions of them living in an area you could drop into Texas and have space left over. But by restraint and politeness, they seemed to get along just fine. That's where he and Susan had gone wrong. She had made a shambles of his apartment, and he hadn't even told her it bothered the hell out of him. He had just gritted his teeth and smiled. And when she left, she had said that odd, bothersome thing: "I want a whole relationship, Matt. A friend, as well as a lover." He had thought he was being considerate, keeping all his dissatisfaction to himself.

Matt admitted he hadn't been an ideal partner, but Cathy would be. And with her to nudge him into line, he was sure he could do better. She wasn't one to sweep any little unpleasantness under the rug. She'd haul it out and make them examine it and cure it.

"What's the matter, did you miss one whisker?" she asked when he came out.

He ran his palm over his cheek. She could almost feel his taut skin, smooth from the razor. "Come and feel for yourself," he tempted.

"I'll take your word for it."

"I didn't offer my word. I suggested you feel for yourself."

She didn't trust the way he was staring at her with that dreamy, sexy look in his eyes. She didn't trust herself to get too close to him, either. "I don't see any stubble."

She picked up her purse and headed for the door with Matt following behind her. "Coward," he said tauntingly over her shoulder. She ignored it and walked a little faster to the elevator.

While the doorman got them a taxi, they peered up and down the street for any sign of Carr. They agreed that if he was there, he was invisible. They were soon deposited at the Lichee Gardens restaurant.

"My mouth starts watering as soon as I see a place like this, with dragons and gilt and silk," Cathy said. "I wonder if I'm part Chinese."

"No, part Japanese," he said obscurely.

"I'm not into sushi."

"We have something in common."

The waiter led them to a table and handed them a menu. "I could eat everything on this," Cathy said after examining it. "Chicken soo guy, sweet-and-sour shrimp, egg rolls—how is a person supposed to decide?"

"I suggest we order the dinner for two, for the variety. We can share each other's dishes."

"What do you like?"

Considerate. This woman really had everything. "This is your night and your dinner. I'll eat whatever you don't want."

"Gee, will just plain rice be enough?" she asked, laughing.

"We'll make it a dinner for three. That way we get two extra dishes. And two extra egg rolls."

"That'll be too much, Matt. My eyes are bigger than my stomach."

"I've noticed you have nice big eyes—with long lashes."

He was starting it again, and since Cathy admitted to herself that she was too susceptible to this line of talk, she tried to derail it. "Just so long as you haven't noticed the size of my pot."

"You don't have a pot," he objected at once. "I would have noticed. I've been looking hard enough."

"Blind in one eye and can't see out of the other. How nice."

"They say love is blind."

Cathy put down the menu and looked at him, frowning. "I've been looking forward to this Chinese dinner for ages, Matt. Don't let's spoil it by arguing about Cleveland. I've never lived with anyone, except my parents, I mean. They're kind of old-fashioned. I guess I am, too. I don't consider my future husband a pair of shoes that I try on to see if they fit and take them back if they pinch a little.'' She saw that little start he gave—what had caused it? Was it the dread *H* word, *husband?*

But it wasn't that. Matt was only surprised at his own perspicacity. He was right! She certainly *did* face problems head-on. No beating around the bush, no pulling her punches. I don't intend to live with you without marriage, she was saying.

It was his turn to speak, and he said without thinking, ''Do you consider me a pair of shoes?''

''It was just a metaphor. What I mean is, no two people are going to be a perfect match. They're bound to have differences. They have to work their problems out. That's all.''

''But I couldn't agree with you more!''

''And if the commitment isn't there, they're not going to work it out. First the commitment, then marriage, then living together. I know it's not for everyone, but it's my way.'' Before he could add to his agreement, she picked up the menu, and said, ''Now, the dinner for two, I think. And let's have some green tea to start.'' Well, that was out of the way! She hoped they had finished with this business of living together.

But when dinner was ordered, Matt returned to the attack. ''I have to admit your way works, Cathy. Your parents have been married for twenty-five years.''

''Yes, and it could easily have gone wrong. They weren't even the same nationality. Mom was a Canadian. They met right here in Toronto. She was a nurse, and Dad broke his leg.'' She told him all the details of the story she had so often heard from her parents.

Matt listened, and when she finished, he said, ''I'd call that a lucky break.''

"That's what they call it, too. How about your parents, Matt?"

"They broke up when I was ten, after a stormy marriage, to say the least. I still remember the arguments." Was that why he avoided confrontations in his relationships? Complaints led to arguments, and arguments led to separation. "I went to live with Mom. She remarried soon after. My stepfather was all right. He didn't beat me or anything. In fact, he spoiled me rotten, as far as material things go, but he thought I was a bloody nuisance. I expect I was, since I resented his breaking up our home."

Strange how he still felt angry and sad and even a little frightened at these memories. The sheer terror of childhood was gone, of course, but the memory stirred something deep inside of him.

Cathy noticed his haunted mood, and said, "Those breakups are hard on the children. It must have been awful."

He shook himself back to the present. "I survived. I never considered him my real father. I went to live with my Dad when I was sixteen and was given the choice. Dad never remarried. He's retired now, living in Florida. I think he still loves Mom. Funny. I doubt she's given him two minutes' thought since the day she left him."

"That's too bad, but you shouldn't let it scare you away from marriage. That's just an objective observation," she added to let him know she wasn't trying to coerce him into anything.

A flashing smile told her he had read her mind. "I didn't take it for a proposal, Cathy. I suppose those early years did influence my views on women and marriage."

"That's probably why you broke up with—what was her name, the woman you lived with?"

"Susan—but I didn't break up with her. She left me."

"She left you!" Cathy exclaimed, shocked. It seemed impossible that any woman would walk out on Matt. "What on earth did you do?"

"I'm beginning to realize it's what I didn't do," he said with a tinge of regret. It seemed bad form to talk about an old flame. He was glad that their dinner arrived to cause a distraction.

For the next half hour, conversation was erratic, mostly raves about the food. Cathy tried not to harp on that tantalizing bit of information he had dropped. Susan—she was wildly curious about this Susan and the fact that she had left Matt. Because of something he didn't do. He wouldn't marry her, was that it? She soon concluded she had found the answer.

"If I didn't have a pot before, I sure will after this," Cathy said when they were breaking open their after-dinner fortune cookies. "What does yours say, Matt?"

He pulled out the little strip of paper. "Confucius say, 'When you have faults, do not fear to abandon them.' Cheeky fellow, this Confucius. Is he suggesting I have a fault? What's yours?"

She opened it, and read, "The cautious seldom err."

"An unnecessary reminder, surely."

She read a hint of laughter in his glinting gaze. So he thought she was too cautious, did he? Personally she considered that warning very apropos at this time. It was reinforcement that she shouldn't let Matt persuade her into something she would regret. "I wouldn't say that."

"You do have your incautious moments, then?"

"Occasionally. I let you barge in at my table for lunch one day—and look at all the trouble that caused."

"Confucius Wilson say, 'Nothing ventured, nothing gained.' You've gained a torn jacket, various assaults on your space and property and a wretch hounding you to death."

"You're not that bad," she joked.

"I meant Carr."

"I know. And speaking of Carr, where do you want to look for him tonight? Is it back to Serge's concert?"

"He won't be there, but I suppose we should look."

"There's an old-time dinner dance at the Royal York. You can go after dinner just for the dance. Does Carr like swing music?"

"It hasn't come up. To dance, he'd need a partner."

"Does he ever see other women?"

"As a matter of fact, he was posing as a widower in Atlantic City and went out with a female dealer a few times. It might be worth a try, since we'll be at the Royal York anyway."

He paid the bill and they went outside. "The hotel's not far. Let's walk off some of that dinner," Cathy suggested.

They strolled hand in hand through the night city, talking when they had anything to say, but familiar enough now to be silent for long stretches, too. Neither one felt any necessity to fill the gaps. As they neared the hotel, Cathy gathered up her courage to ask about Susan. "What did Susan do for a job?" she inquired first, from which she hoped to get more-personal details.

"She was a secretary. She worked in the same building as me. We met in the coffee shop."

"Oh," was all she said. She had thought Susan would be a model or actress or someone glamorous.

"She's married now. It was a few years ago."

"That's too bad. I guess you really loved her, huh?"

He smiled down at her. "I thought I did. I was pretty immature. Great dinner, wasn't it?" he said, quickly changing the subject.

"Fabulous."

"A delightful meal." He cocked his head at an angle and said, "The food wasn't bad, either."

It seemed impossible to revert to Susan after that. Matt obviously didn't want to discuss her.

Chapter Eight

The crowd at Alceze's concert was bigger than it had been the night before. Every table was taken, the bar stools were all full and a throng of classical-guitar fans stood at the rear of the room, listening. Matt and Cathy joined the standing group and examined the room. At the end of the set, Matt asked, "Have you seen anything?"

Cathy shook her head. "He's not here, but it's early yet. He may come later."

"Let's take a peek in at the dinner dance."

The busy waiters hadn't served them yet, so they worked their way out into the lobby and went to the Imperial Room. Here the room was larger, but the tables were well spaced and the crowd thinner. It didn't take long to see that Carr wasn't there.

"This doesn't look like his sort of place," Matt said. "Too polite. He'd be more at home in a dark bar, or in a smoke-filled room, playing poker. I wonder where the illicit gambling is carried on in town."

"You could ask a cabdriver," she suggested. "They're supposed to know things like that."

"There are probably a dozen places, and it'd be hit-and-miss whether I found the right one. Arrangements have to be made before you're let in, too. You don't just knock on the door, unless you want a gun aimed at your nose."

They took another look around the bar before returning to Cathy's hotel. The happy mood of dinner had dissipated as they looked in vain for Carr. It wasn't late, but Cathy was tired and was glad to get back.

"I'll go up to your room with you just to make sure everything's all right there," Matt said while they waited for the elevator.

"I can look after myself. I'm a cop." His tolerant smile, suggesting that handling Carr was a man's job, rankled. Yet she appreciated his company.

"You're not packing your gun, though. I'll give Reilly a buzz from your room and see if anything happened at the Plaza while I was away."

"Aren't you going back there now?" she asked.

He gave a conscious look. "Yes, pretty soon."

"As soon as you've spoken to a cabdriver and visited a few gambling dens," she said, shaking her head. "That's pretty dangerous, Matt."

A man and woman got into the elevator with them, making it impossible for them to continue their conversation. When the couple got out at the fifth floor, Matt said, "I'd just hang around outside till Carr came out—if he came out. I don't intend to crash the game."

"Just as well. You don't exactly have a poker face. I knew you were up to something."

The elevator stopped, and they continued to her room. Matt felt a little disappointed that she didn't try to dissuade him. "It could be dangerous," he mentioned, peering for her reaction.

"You'd better be careful," was all she said. Danger had always been a part of her family's life. Her mother had accepted it and learned to live with it. Nagging didn't help.

She unlocked the door and they entered. "Hotel rooms smell so stuffy," she said. "I'd rather have fresh air than this dull air-conditioned smell. If you want to call Reilly, go ahead. Everything seems to be all right here." She glanced around the room, checking to see that nothing had been disarranged.

"I'll have a glass of water first," Matt said. "Alcohol leaves my throat dry." He went into the bathroom and unwrapped a glass. He reached for the tap to let it run to make sure the water was cold. His hand stopped. There, in the sink, was a little disk of cigarette ash. Cathy didn't smoke; he didn't smoke, but Carr did. Cathy had mentioned the stale air in the room. He'd noticed it himself. Cigarette smoke lingered awhile, even with an air conditioner.

Rage was his usual reaction when Carr outwitted him, but on this occasion fear was added to it. My God, Carr walked in and out of their private rooms as if he were a ghost, passing through solid walls. How had he found them? How had he gotten in? There wasn't a single doubt in Matt's mind that the caller who left the ash was Carr. And it was entirely possible that he'd return when Cathy was alone. Matt didn't want to frighten her, but he couldn't leave her alone. He'd have to stay the night—and that presented problems.

"Matt," Cathy called from the bedroom. He noticed the apprehensive tone of her voice and hurried out.

She stood by the desk, looking down at the wastebasket. In her hand she held a small slip of paper. "Am I crazy, or is this the bill from that book on Moore you bought the other day at the gallery?"

He took the bill and examined it. "This is it. Why?"

"I found it on the chair, here at this desk. I was using it for a bookmark in the book. I haven't opened the book since I moved to this room. I haven't even taken it out of the suitcase. How did it get here?"

"Come with me, and I'll show you how," he said. He took her elbow and led her to the sink. "That's how," he said, pointing at the ash in the sink. "We've had company while we were out."

Her heart clenched in fear and anger. "Carr! Does he smoke?" she demanded.

"Yes. I'm not Sherlock Holmes. I don't have a laboratory with me to analyze this bit of ash, but I'd bet ten to one Carr dropped it."

"And he was riffling through my things, looking for the film—or maybe pictures, since a film obviously wasn't concealed in a book." Anger swelled, driving out the fear. "The nerve of him! Who does he think he is, sneaking into my room every time my back is turned? How does he even know we're here? We didn't see a sign of him when we left the Plaza."

"There are so many people hanging around the lobbies of big hotels that it's easy for one man to hide. He was probably wearing a disguise. All he had to do was rush out after we left the Plaza and ask the doorman where we went. Say we had forgotten something, and he wanted to follow us to return it."

"But I registered under my mother's name. How could he know this was my room?"

"He must have darted up to the registration desk as soon as you left it and registered under some other name. In that way, he'd get a look at your room number."

"Then you think he's here in this hotel?" she asked, eyes sparkling angrily.

Matt thought about it a moment. "He wouldn't necessarily book the room. Maybe he just inquired."

"Maybe he did register, since he's obviously hanging around here somewhere nearby."

"That's possible," he conceded.

A banked fire glowed in her eyes, giving her the air of a predatory cat. "If he is staying here, we can find out what room he's in and get him."

"What do you mean?" he asked warily.

"You said he probably signed in right after me—if he signed in, that is. It's worth a shot to look at the hotel registry and see whose name is under mine. If it's someone with the initials J.C., we'll know. Now, how can we do it? Maybe if you speak to the hotel detective, Matt . . ."

"Good thinking! I'll give him a ring."

Cathy was pleased with her quick thinking and with Matt's approval. He went to the phone, and within a few minutes there was a tap at the door. The man who entered was the same general type as John Reilly. He was tall, well muscled, and didn't stand out in any way. Cathy knew these were qualifications for the job of hotel detective, that you were husky and looked fairly anonymous. Ex-policemen often applied for this softer job when they grew weary with the force. Her dad, when he was in a bad mood, sometimes threatened to do it, but of course he never would.

"I'm Harry Hunter, hotel security," the man said. "What's this all about, folks?"

Matt explained and suggested that Harry phone John Reilly at the Plaza to check their story. "I'll just do that. I know John. We were on the force together five years ago."

"Ask him if Carr showed up while you're at it," Matt said.

Harry dialed, and said, "John, Harry Hunter here. I'm with a guy called Wilson and a lady friend. They say you know them?" He talked a few minutes to Reilly. When he hung up, he said, "You didn't have any visitors, but Reilly figures Carr was still interested. You got two phone calls. When Reilly answered, the guy hung up. If it was a guy. He didn't say anything at all."

"He was checking to see if anyone was in the room," Cathy said. "Will you check the registry for us and see who signed in right after me? I used the name Mona Hardy." She explained her reason for doing so to the detective.

Harry made another call, this time to the desk. "A Jonathon Coates," he said, hanging up. Matt and Cathy exchanged a satisfied look.

"It's got to be him!" Matt exclaimed. "He usually keeps his initials."

"Room 724. That's just down the hall. Shall we drop in on him?" Hunter suggested, smiling in anticipation. He patted a bulge beneath his shoulder. Of course the house detective would have a gun.

Matt gave an apprehensive glance at Cathy. "You'd better stay here. There might be trouble," he said.

"I intend to add to the trouble," she shot back, fire in her eyes. "I owe Carr a few kicks."

"It'd be better if you stay here, ma'am, and keep an eye on the elevator in case he comes while we're in his room," Mr. Hunter said. He smiled at her disappointed expression, and added, "If we get him, we'll bring him here after we disarm him and let you have a go at him." He turned to Matt. "You all set?"

"Ready and waiting."

Cathy kept an eye on the elevator. How was she supposed to let them know if Carr did come? Would she have time to phone? Hunter had just used that as a pretext to keep her out of harm! She watched in uncertainty as Hunter and Matt turned the corner at the end of the hall and disappeared from view.

Matt's heart hammered in anticipation as they approached the door. Eight months' work was about to come to fruition. Carr had outwitted him for the last time. He'd put that scoundrel behind bars and get on with his life. He had some vacation coming up. Maybe he and Cathy could...

Hunter tapped on the door politely. There was no answer. He tapped harder, then a third time. When there was still no answer, he used his passkey and opened the door. It was completely dark inside. If Carr were there waiting, he'd have a clear shot at a lit target. Hunter moved aside to protect his body by the wall, and reached his long arm in to flick on the light. The room appeared not only empty but as if no one had been in it since the maid had cleaned it.

He entered, carefully hugging the side of the wall. It was soon clear that Carr wasn't there. They examined the room. The ashtrays held a few butts and ashes. One of the glasses in the bathroom had been used. There was an indentation on the bedspread, as if someone had lounged there for a while. Other than that, the room was undisturbed.

"He spent a bit of time here, but he didn't bring any luggage. There's no guarantee he'll ever come back. He paid cash, for one night," Hunter said. "We do get a few old-timers who don't trust plastic, so the desk didn't make anything of it. I could get a set of prints from that glass he used."

"Maybe you'd better. Not that it'll do any good. His prints aren't on record. They didn't print newborn babies in the hospital fifty years ago. This is his first major-league plunge into crime."

"You must have got prints from his house and effects."

"By the time we smelled a rat and started investigating, his loving widow had cleaned and dusted and polished and scoured everything he ever touched. She also managed to lose any pictures of him. We have no prints, and the only sample of his handwriting we have is on his insurance policy. He had a cut finger the day he signed, self-inflicted, of course, to make the signature useless for comparison."

"He's a thorough rascal, isn't he?" Hunter said, impressed.

"He's either a genius or a demon." Matt sighed, defeated once again.

"He might come back here," Mr. Hunter said.

"It's possible, but I doubt it. He moves quickly. What'll happen is that the key for the room, carefully wiped of prints, will be in the mail. That way, no questions arise."

"Do you have a picture of him?" Hunter asked. "I'll keep an eye out for him in the lobby."

Matt took out his picture. It had faded beyond recognition. Like the Cheshire cat, only the ghost of a smile remained. "No, I don't have one. Carr is lucky, as well as clever."

"Some days you can't make a nickel," Hunter said.

"I do have a sketch of him at my hotel. You can ask Reilly to send it over."

"I'll do that. It always helps to know who you're looking for."

"He might be in disguise, of course," Matt mentioned.

"I'd better be getting along. If you want me, just call the desk. I have to earn my keep. Things are pretty quiet here at the hotel, but I have to make my rounds. You won't be leaving the young lady alone in that room?"

"No, I won't."

Hunter gave an ambiguous laugh and left. Matt returned to Cathy's room and told the story. She settled herself comfortably on one of the beds, while Matt sat on the chair by the desk.

She listened avidly, and when he was finished, she said, "He might come back to the room. If he's dumb or desperate enough to think I still have the film, he must think it's in my purse. So far, he's only sneaked in when I'm not here. He might make one last effort while I'm asleep." It didn't take her long to realize that this placed her in some peril. "I'd suggest changing rooms, or hotels, except that Carr seems to know exactly where we go," she added. "I wish

Dad were here. He'd know what to do. He has years of experience. I'm still a rookie.''

Matt was offended at this oblique hint that he didn't know what he was doing, but as it was so well deserved, he didn't overreact. "I know what to do. The thing is, you won't like it.''

She read the uncertainty on his face. "You stay here with me, you mean?'' she asked. It had already occurred to her as the safest solution, so far as any danger from Carr went. The trouble was, it brought with it other perils, such as the presence overnight in her bedroom under intimate circumstances of the man she was falling in love with. She cast an apprehensive look at Matt.

He was surprised and relieved that the idea had come from her. At least he didn't have to suggest it now and rouse her defenses. "I'm perfectly willing to stay,'' he offered, trying to conceal his relief.

"Fortunately there are two beds,'' she said calmly, but she took a peek at Matt as she said it and mistrusted the look of surprise on his face. Had he taken for granted they'd share not only the room, but a bed?

"I was afraid I'd have to sleep in the bathtub,'' he said, chewing back a smile.

"That'd be silly,'' she scoffed. "We might as well make the best of a bad situation.''

The situation hadn't seemed that bad to Matt, but he went along with her to soothe her fears. "It's unfortunate, but really it seems the sane course. And, of course, Hunter will be on the lookout below. Reilly's sending the sketch of Carr over for Hunter to see what he looks like.''

She lounged back against the stacked pillows on the bed. "Doesn't it just make your blood boil that we're stuck here worrying, while he's probably out enjoying himself?''

Matt answered with feeling. "I've been going through this for months. My only petty revenge is that I've kept the company from settling the insurance claim. They can't hold off much longer."

There was a long evening ahead of them, and Cathy decided to try to learn more about Matt. "Is this the only case you're working on, Matt?"

"At the moment, yes. When the claim is so large, they assign an agent full-time. It's worth the company's while. If I succeed, I save them a bundle."

"What other sorts of cases do you have?" she asked to try to get an idea of his life.

"Oh, accident victims who claim they're crippled for life. I spy around and see if I can catch them playing tennis or jogging. We get quite a few stolen or lost jewelry claims. If we suspect the client's story, I try to find who they sold the stuff to or where they've hidden it. Things like that."

"It sounds interesting."

"It's pretty dangerous, of course," he pointed out, hoping for some display of concern.

"Yes," she said blandly. "So's my and Dad's line of work. I guess I'm used to that aspect of it." She glanced at her watch. It wasn't quite eleven yet. She knew she wouldn't sleep and didn't particularly relish the thought of tossing and turning restlessly for hours with Matt close enough to hear every move.

"Shall we see what's on TV?" she suggested.

"Sure, why should Carr have all the fun?" he asked ironically. They watched the news first, then stayed tuned to see what late movie was on.

"A Western," she said. She didn't like Westerns, but thought Matt would probably enjoy it.

Matt looked at her uncertainly. He didn't want to see it, either, but thought she might. "Shall we watch it?" he asked.

"If you want to." She perused the TV guide and saw that a mystery thriller was on another channel.

"Anything else on?" he asked.

She mentioned the thriller, looking for his reaction.

He took her uncertainty for reluctance. "Let's watch the Western," he said, feigning enthusiasm.

For five minutes they listened, bored, to horses galloping and guns roaring. "I'll just close my eyes and rest," he said. "I think I've seen this one."

"Oh, well, if you're not going to watch it, I'll change the channel. I'd prefer the mystery. It might help me in my work. Never know when you might learn a new trick."

Matt watched her, then a slow smile crept across his lips. "You don't like shoot-em-ups, either, huh? I was just trying to be polite."

"Me, too." She laughed. "That'll teach us to be so darned considerate."

"I misread you. I figured you always spoke your mind."

"I usually do," she said, wondering why she had refrained on this occasion. Was she trying to be agreeable so Matt would like her? Nothing wrong with being considerate, but it didn't always work out. "It lasts till one-thirty," she mentioned. "Is that too late for you?"

"Nope. Now, if we just had a tub of popcorn..."

"I doubt if room service supplies that, but there's a candy machine in the hall. Shall we stock up?"

"Better make it snappy. We don't want to miss the beginning."

They riffled through pockets and purse to assemble all their change. The had enough for a can of soda, as well as two candy bars each. "Great, a pig-out!" Cathy laughed as they ran back to their room. "I don't know how we'll find room for it, after that huge dinner."

"I guess it's true what they say about Chinese food. An hour later you're hungry again."

She didn't object when Matt shared her bed. Hers had a better view of the screen. They kicked off their shoes, stacked their pillows and settled in for the evening.

The movie was an intriguing murder mystery. The beautiful heroine was being menaced by someone and taking steps to kill her predator before he killed her. They watched silently while the film played, completely engrossed in the story. During the commercial breaks they discussed the plot and characters.

"I think it's her husband who's trying to kill her," Cathy said. "He's the only one who'd benefit."

"No, the other way around. He's the one who has the insurance policy, and she's the beneficiary," he pointed out.

"Count on you to keep track of insurance. She has money herself. And she's the one who got the knockout drink."

"She could have given herself the drink to make him look suspicious." Matt glanced impatiently at his watch. "What's taking them so long to get back to the movie? They get you hooked, then blast commercials in every two minutes."

"Here it is now," Cathy said.

"That's a beautiful heroine," Matt said, easing himself luxuriously back against the pillows.

For no particular reason, Cathy thought of Susan and felt a definite sense of irritation. "She looks cheap with those painted eyebrows," she sniffed. She knew it was crazy to be jealous of a movie star, but the actress was certainly beautiful. If this was the kind of woman Matt liked, he must find her a mouse.

Matt enjoyed watching the actress, but that was not the thing he enjoyed most about the evening. What he liked was just being alone together with Cathy, as if they were at home, relaxing. He was glad they liked the same things. It was fun to go out on the town, too, but sometimes a person just wanted to goof off and watch TV.

As the movie reached its chilling climax, Matt felt Cathy's hand move uncertainly into his. "I hope he isn't going to kill her!" she said, her eyes wide with apprehension.

On the screen the couple appeared to be stalking each other in an empty house. Matt didn't remember how they'd gotten there. His mind must have been wandering. He felt protective with Cathy's small hand curled trustingly in his. What had he been thinking of, involving Cathy in such danger as she was in from Carr? If anything happened to her...

His heart was pounding heavily in his chest. He loved her! That was what had happened to him. He *must* love her, because if anything happened to Cathy Auden, he knew he'd never forgive himself and never get over it. He saw her wiping surreptitiously at a tear. She was the sort of sentimental woman who cried at movies. Tenderhearted. The movie was over. He wanted to cradle her in his arms and kiss her tears away, but if he allowed himself the luxury, he was afraid he wouldn't be able to control himself.

"It's only a movie, Cathy," he said gently. "It's one-thirty. We should be getting to bed."

She turned her head aside to hide the ignominy of red eyes. She was a cop, for heaven's sake! She shouldn't be bawling at a movie. "You go ahead and use the bathroom first," she said.

As soon as he was gone, she began to worry about the sleeping arrangements. What was Matt going to wear to bed, for instance? Were his pajamas in his suitcase? Was he going to lie three feet away from her in nothing but his underwear? Would he even wear that? And she hadn't brought a housecoat with her. She'd hired a private room for the tour, so she hadn't thought she'd need one, and the housecoat took up so much space in her bag that she'd left it at home. She'd have to make the dash from bathroom to bed in a flimsy, short nightie, with Matt watching. Would it look too prudish to ask him to turn out the light?

And what if he tried to climb into her bed during the night? She really didn't know him well enough to know what he might do under the prevailing circumstances, although he certainly hadn't made any moves on her during the whole two hours of the movie. Her father would think she was insane if he knew she was sharing a bedroom with a man she scarcely knew. She *was* insane. Matt could overpower her easily. Yet the alternative, that he wasn't attracted enough to her to even suggest anything, was depressing, too.

She heard the water running, and before she had her thoughts straightened out, Matt came out. He was fully dressed. ''Your turn,'' he said nonchalantly. If he planned to try anything, he certainly wasn't betraying it.

She went into the bathroom, snatching up her nightie on the way. Maybe he was out there, totally naked, waiting in the dark for her. Goose bumps lifted the hair on her arms as she watched the water run down into the sink. She got out her toothbrush, gave her teeth a quick brush, washed her face and decided that was enough cleanliness for now. She undressed and put on her nightie, then threw a bath towel over her shoulders for the trip to her bed.

When she eased the door open, she saw that Matt had turned off all the lights except the lamp by her bedside. The room was dim, but not dark. She managed to keep her pace to a dignified walk, instead of a betraying gallop. She glanced at the other bed and saw Matt's naked shoulders protruding above the sheet. Taut muscles gleamed silver in the shadows. A patch of dark on his chest caught her attention. Presumably he had removed his trousers. Well, at least he was in his own bed, and his eyes were closed, though of course he couldn't possibly be asleep yet. Thoughtful of him to give her some privacy.

When Matt heard her bedsprings squawk, he said, "Can I open my eyes now?"

Cathy hastily pulled the sheet up around her neck. "Sure. I'm just going to turn out the light."

Her voice sounded breathless, and Matt was sensitive enough to have some idea what was bothering her. He wanted to reassure her, but to even mention the sexual possibilities implicit in their situation seemed crude. He said, "Good night, Cathy."

"Good night, Matt," she replied, and turned out the light.

They both lay as silent and rigid as corpses, though each was acutely aware of the other's close proximity. Cathy hardly even breathed, for fear of keeping him awake. The best thing that could possibly happen was for him to go to sleep immediately and not awaken until daylight. Daylight was safe. It was being together in this dark room that bothered her. She should have put the can of Mace under her pillow. She moved her hand outside the sheet, feeling on the floor for her purse. Of course it was nowhere within reach. She remembered seeing it on the desk when they'd come back from buying the soda pop and candy. If she heard him move off the bed, she'd make a dash for her purse.

But he didn't seem to be making any noise at all. He was certainly a quiet sleeper. She wondered where Carr was and if they'd have a visit from him during the night. Maybe they should have put a desk in front of the door or something. Matt couldn't possibly be asleep yet. Should she mention it to him? No, she wouldn't sleep tonight. If she heard anything, that would be time enough to awaken him.

"Cathy." The word, though quietly spoken, sounded as ominous as thunder in her ears.

She didn't answer for a moment. Was this it? Was he going to suggest he share her bed. Her body stiffened like a frozen sheet in the wind. "What?" she asked in a strained voice.

"Don't be frightened." Her heart leapt into her throat. "I'm going to get up and put a chair under the doorknob in case Carr comes. I'm a light sleeper. I'll hear him and maybe catch him. I just thought I should tell you why I'm getting out of bed. Okay?"

She felt weak with relief. "Sure, Matt. I was just thinking the same thing myself."

"Great minds think alike," he said in a very ordinary voice. He didn't turn on any lights, perhaps because he was wearing only his underwear. She listened while he got the chair, arranged it under the knob and returned to bed. "Good night," he said again.

"Good night, Matt."

The minor incident reassured her. That was thoughtful of him, telling her why he was getting out of bed in case she was frightened. He was really a nice guy. He wouldn't take advantage of their situation. He'd had two constant days of her company to misbehave, if that was what he had in mind. He probably didn't even find her attractive. No, that wasn't it. He had more or less suggested they live together, so he must like her, even if she wasn't exactly his preferred type.

Her eyelids fluttered closed, and soon Matt heard the light, measured breaths of sleep. Well, thank God Cathy was getting some sleep, anyway, because he was darned sure he wasn't going to close an eye all night. How could he sleep, with that gorgeous, desirable woman not five feet away from him? He had never wanted anyone so badly in his life, but Cathy was different—special. Things had to be done right with a woman like that. First love, then marriage, then living together, she'd said. That suited him fine. What he had to do now was convince her he wasn't just some guy on the make, then he had to convince her that she loved him. And he had all of one or two days in which to accomplish it.

Chapter Nine

Matt awoke first. As his memory focused and the strange surroundings became familiar, his eyes darted to the door. The chair was in place, so everything was all right. He looked over to the other bed and saw a tousle of chestnut curls on the pillow, unmoving. His wary expression softened to tenderness. Cathy's slow and regular breaths told him she was still asleep. He wanted to slip quietly over and gaze at her, but it seemed an imposition. Instead, he crawled out of bed, careful to make the minimum of noise, and put on his shirt and trousers.

Running an exploratory hand over his jaw, he felt the rough stubble of an incipient beard. With his dark hair, it showed clearly. He didn't have a razor and he didn't want Cathy to see him like this. What he really wanted was a shower and change of clothes, but that would have to wait till he could get to his own hotel. He tiptoed, with elaborate precautions against noise, to the telephone and lifted the receiver. He asked for two cups of coffee, the morning paper and a razor.

Until the tap came at the door, he just stood, thinking. Today was the day. He either encountered Carr at the antique market, or had to come up with another plan to find him. He felt he should hang around Toronto a few more days, then maybe a quick dash back to Atlantic City. He'd see Cathy safely on her flight home on Sunday morning. If he caught Carr today, this evening would be a magnificent celebration. And if he didn't ... He glanced again toward Cathy's bed. They'd celebrate anyway. The gentle, anticipatory smile looked incongruous on his unshaven face.

Was it too soon to propose to her? Would she think he was crazy? And most importantly, would she accept him? He regretted that he'd ever suggested living together. That might be enough to finish his chances. He didn't want her to just fly away home and forget all about him.

He went to the door, removed the chair and watched through the peephole for room service so the porter wouldn't knock on the door and awaken her. When the man came, Matt took one cup of coffee to Cathy's bedside and placed it on the table beside her. It made a good excuse to do what he'd been wanting to do—look at her. Just look at her a moment with her face relaxed in sleep. He set the coffee down and stood, gazing, while something inside of him turned to marshmallow.

She slept on her side with one arm under her pillow, the other out over the sheet. He admired her delicate, long-fingered hand with shell pink nails. A strand of hair curled round her neck, nestling under chin. He resisted the urge to push it back. Beneath the strand the gleam of her golden wishbone on its slender chain caught his attention. A girlish aberration, that. She wasn't superstitious. She was an intelligent, levelheaded woman. Long eyelashes fanned in twin arcs over her cheeks. She looked sweet and vulnerable and about twelve years old. He knew that it was an image he would carry forever, etched into memory. He stifled the urge to reach down and kiss her forehead.

He took the razor into the bathroom, carefully closed the door and performed the quietest shave of his life. The water barely trickled from the tap to lessen the noise. When he came out, he tripped over his own shoes, and an exclamation escaped from his lips.

Cathy leapt up from her pillow, staring in fright. In the dark edges of the room, she saw the outline of a man, and her surprise congealed to instant terror. Then her eyes alit on her purse, and she gauged her chances of reaching it before the man—Carr—caught her.

"Sorry, Cathy," the dark shadow said apologetically. Matt! Her confusion was complete. "I tripped. There's a cup of coffee on your bedside table."

"Matt!" she said, and collapsed, giggling, in the aftermath of her fright. She remembered then her foolish terrors of the night before. "You scared the life out of me," she said, reaching for the coffee. "Thanks." She lifted the cup in salute. "And good morning. I see we made it through the night unmolested. By Carr, I mean!" she added quickly.

"But of course," he replied with a sapient smile. "Who else could you mean?"

She was glad he hadn't taken offense. While Matt went to get his coffee, she hastily arranged the top sheet around her in some semblance of modesty. He drew the desk chair near her pillow, and said, "No jiggles at the door during the night. Since you're awake, it might be a good idea for us to nip over to my hotel before Carr is up and about. I have to shower and change."

"So do I."

"I'll stand guard for you," he said, smiling.

He looked so harmless in the light of morning that she couldn't imagine what she'd been frightened of the night before. She had done him an injustice. Matt obviously had no designs of that sort on her. Then the troublesome question obtruded—didn't he find her attractive, now that he was coming to know her better?

"How's the coffee?" he asked.

"Just right. How did you know I take cream and no sugar?"

"You sound as if we're strangers!" he exclaimed. "We've shared several cups of coffee. I keep my eyes and ears open. I know a lot about you by now."

"Just little things that don't really matter," she said dismissingly.

"I know about your parents, where they met, what they do, how long they've been married. I even know your mother, Mona's, maiden name. I know you think a lot of them and are a thoughtful, dutiful daughter. I know you have a kid brother who likes Wolfe. Rob, isn't it? I know the hospital where you were born, the house where you were raised. I know what your job is. And since you're clever and industrious, I suspect you're good at it. I know you like Chinese food and mystery movies, and have old-fa—er, traditional views on love and marriage."

"All right, I'm convinced," she said, laughing. "Stop, before you get to my bad features."

"I don't think you have any—except stubbornness," he added. His dreamy look suggested that was his favorite fault.

"I call it determination."

"I call it stubborn," he repeated.

"I won't continue this pointless argument—that would be stubborn. Actually you know a lot more about me than I know about you."

He lifted his eyebrows and chided playfully, "Maybe that's because I'm more the more interested of the two."

"Or maybe it's because I'm a blabbermouth and you keep things to yourself."

"You know something about my background. I told you my parents were divorced." Why had he told her that? He never told it to any other woman he was interested in. Was it an unconscious bid for sympathy, an excuse for his exploits?

"I don't even know where you were born or whether you have any brothers or sisters."

"Chicago, and I'm an only child. I have few secrets. Just enough to keep a lady interested, I hope." She watched as the playfulness evaporated and a steady, inscrutable gaze settled on her. "I'll be happy to tell you anything you want to know, but let's save it for later. Time for your shower now. I know you're modest—I read minds, as well as actions," he said, his eyes just glancing off the sheet she held tightly around her chest. "So I'll stick my nose in the newspaper while you grab your clothes and streak into the bathroom."

He picked up his coffee, took the newspaper and went to the desk, where he turned on the lamp and lifted the paper high in front of his eyes.

Cathy gathered up her clothes and hurried into the bathroom for her shower. She was growing fonder of this Matt Wilson by the minute. In fact, she felt guilty for having mistrusted him the night before. She wouldn't be so standoffish today. While the warm water pelted her back and shoulders, she cast her mind forward to their day. They'd have to find out when the antique market opened. It could be a long day if it opened in the morning and lasted till evening. But it wouldn't be dull with Matt there to talk to and laugh with.

She didn't know as many facts about his background as he had somehow found out about hers, but she was beginning to learn what kind of man he was. He called her stubborn, but he was as stubborn as a mule if he'd been working this hard for the better part of a year to catch Carr. He was hardworking, but he knew how to enjoy life, too. He was fun to be with and thoughtful and dependable. A man you could trust. That was really important.

She felt she could be happy with him, but what she didn't know was how he felt about her and about marriage. He apparently was interested enough to have suggested that they live together, but that was only sexual attraction. That was nice, too, but it wasn't enough. His family background could explain his aversion to marriage, and his fear of long-term commitment. He knew she wasn't interested in anything else, so far as a relationship went. Was that why he had backed off—from her and Susan?

His thoughtfulness last night and this morning showed that he respected her, but respect wasn't love. It was one of the necessary ingredients, though. The real pity of it was that with only one more day of her holidays left, she wasn't going to have time to find out what she wanted to know.

She toweled herself dry, dressed in a shirt and slacks and did a quick job on her face—a daub of lipstick, a hint of rose-colored gel to highlight her cheeks and a feathery line beneath her bottom lashes. A few strokes of the brush tossed her hair back from her face in petaled layers, and she was ready.

Matt was pacing the room when she came out. "All set?" he asked. His eyes made a quick, approving tour from her head to toes. He lifted her straw hat from the desk and dropped it on her head.

"Where's yours?" she asked.

"Mine looks stupid. Yours looks good. I'm leaving mine here, since it obviously didn't fool Carr."

He took her arm and they left. "Should you speak to Mr. Hunter before we leave?" she asked.

"He's off duty now, but I phoned the day man while you were showering. I doubt Carr will come back here. He's already checked out your room."

He had other things he wanted to say to Cathy, but they might upset her, and he meant to wait until after breakfast. No one liked receiving bad news on an empty stomach. They took a cab to the Park Plaza. "Why don't I order us breakfast while you get changed?" she suggested.

Matt's reaction surprised her. He took her hand and put it under his arm. "I don't want to let you out of my sight. Not too far out of it, at least. Do you mind waiting in my room while I have a quick shower? I won't be long."

"I didn't know you cared," she joked.

His reaction to that surprised her, too. He looked surprised. "Then it's time you found out, Miss Auden."

She had plenty to think about while he was in the bathroom. When he came out, she just looked, with a dull ache inside. Matt looked so good she wanted to throw herself into his arms and hang on forever. His crisp black hair was still moist. It clung to his well-shaped head and glistened in the sunlight. The clean, strong lines of his face gave an impression of strength and integrity. Then he smiled, and said, "Ten minutes by the clock. Not bad. You took half an hour."

"I didn't know it was a race." It bothered her that Matt's attitude had changed so dramatically. When they knew each other less well, he used to flirt. He had even suggested they cohabit. Now that she was falling in love with him, he had suddenly turned into this pattern of rectitude. He didn't flirt; he hardly touched her if he could help it.

"It wasn't. I just didn't want to keep you waiting too long. You've just learned something else about me, if you're interested. I'm considerate."

"And modest."

"But of course. Also hungry. Shall we go?"

Nothing could develop in a public dining room. "We could have room service," she said as a sort of test to see if he wanted to be alone with her. "That way, we'll be here if Carr shows up."

Her idea appealed to him—too much. It definitely wasn't a good idea to have long periods of intimacy with Cathy. "We'll have advance notice if we're downstairs. You can see the lobby from the restaurant. Let's go."

Nothing that a sensible person could take exception to occurred over breakfast. Matt was amusing and friendly. He told her an exciting story about his last case. It involved a supposedly stolen Dégas painting. Matt had found out the alleged victim had been in debt, and mysteriously paid off his debt before the insurance company reimbursed him for the painting. "The man had obviously sold it and faked a burglary," he explained.

The case had involved a trip to Paris and dealing with a shady gallery operator. Matt had posed as a connoisseur and during the case exposed a chain of thieves and smugglers. She felt she ought to make more fuss about it, but her heart wasn't in it. It was a story he might have told to just anyone. It had no personal overtones.

"I see you're underwhelmed by my cunning," he said when she made some perfunctory comment.

"It was really clever of you, Matt. I'm just thinking about Carr," she said to have some excuse for her mood.

"That's a nice, discreet way of recalling me to duty. Right. It's time to hit the antique market. I hope you're wearing comfortable shoes."

"I thought you noticed things," she said.

"That's what I get for blowing my own horn. I was too busy noticing your big, beautiful green eyes to look at your feet."

It was too little, and too late. "Actually my eyes are hazel," she retorted, and got up before Matt had time to help her.

He rose and gazed deeply into them. "You're right. They do have gold flecks. But I was right about the beautiful."

On this promising speech, he turned and left the restaurant. Harbourfront was far enough away that they decided to take a cab. "I want you to stick close to me at all times," Matt said.

"Don't worry, I'll protect you."

He ignored this jibe and continued in a serious vein. It was time to give her the bad news. "The thing is, Cathy, you might be in some danger. Carr seems to have latched onto the idea that you have the film. He didn't find it in either search of your hotel room, so the next logical step is to search you—if you get my meaning."

"You mean that would require submission on my part, maybe like my being knocked unconscious?"

"No moss growing on you. I see you understand the situation. I'd ask you to stay at the hotel, but that doesn't seem to be entirely safe, either. Besides, you wouldn't stay there. Your stubbornness, which you stubbornly insist on calling determination, would lead you down to the antique market on your own. At least this way I'm along to protect you."

"You're right, I certainly wouldn't stay locked up in a room all day. But shouldn't we wear some disguise in case he gets a glimpse of us— No, he won't run. He'll hang around and make a try for my purse."

"And I'll be right beside you. If you'd rather not—"

"Of course I'll go!" she said at once. "I'm not afraid of Jim Carr. I'm dying to get my hands on him."

Matt stopped the cab a block from the market. They walked the rest of the way, hand in hand in the sunlight, enjoying the lake and the breeze and the throng of people headed for the market. An interest in antiques wasn't restricted to any particular age or either sex, to judge by the motley crew wending their way to the market. There was everything from teenagers, bouncing along in rhythm to their portable cassette players, to Yuppies in designer shirts and jackets, to old men and women, hobbling along with the aid of canes. Street vendors were hawking hot dogs and ice cream and soft drinks. The air was full of odors and noise, reminding Cathy of carnivals her father had taken her to when she was young. A van with the doors open was doing a brisk business in printed T-shirts.

Cathy bought one for her brother, Rob. It said Toronto and had a picture of the new Skydome, with the CN Tower soaring beside it. They wandered around like tourists, stopping at the outdoor stalls and examining the wares, especially old silver. They kept looking around in all directions for Carr as they strolled.

They reluctantly left the sunlit street and entered the mall. Matt had some interest in old books, and when he stopped at a stall, Cathy wandered along to the next booth, which sold antique jewelry. "I'll be right over there," she said before leaving, as Matt kept stressing the need for staying together.

She looked at the old English engagement rings, wondering if her mother would like one for her anniversary. Her mother had often mentioned preferring them to the conventional diamond engagement ring. Her dad had been short of money when they got engaged, and her mother didn't have a diamond. She asked to see one that caught her eye. It was a wide, embossed gold band with tiny seed pearls interspersed with chips of ruby across the top. She slipped it on her finger. It was very pretty, but when she asked the price, she realized she couldn't afford it.

Matt suddenly appeared at her shoulder. She knew he wouldn't forsake her for long. "That's a pretty thing," he said, looking at her finger.

"It's an engagement ring."

"It doesn't look like one. It doesn't even have a diamond," he said, looking questioningly at her.

"Diamond engagement rings used to be for the rich. This is what average ladies used to wear in England. I was thinking of buying it for Mom."

"Thinking of getting engaged to her, are you?" he joked.

"Dad beat me to it. It's pretty, though, isn't it?"

"Do you like it?" He took a look all around as he spoke.

Cathy knew he was looking for Carr and didn't resent his apparent lack of attention to her. "I love it, but it's beyond my limited resources. Did you find any interesting books?" She removed the ring and put it back in the case.

"I found a first-edition Hemingway, signed. They're asking five bucks for it."

"That sounds like a bargain, Matt!"

"Signed in red crayon, and 'Ernest' was spelled wrong. They added an *a*. Somehow I don't think Ernest used a red crayon. Some kid had scribbled through the book. Pity. Would you like to see it?"

She went to the book counter with him, and he showed her the page with the childish scrawl in red. Cathy spotted a copy of *Anne of Green Gables* and leafed through it. She already had a copy, but this one was much older and had pictures. She flipped through it for a minute. Soon she looked up to scan the horizon for Carr. When she turned to speak to Matt, he had wandered off. Of course, he hadn't gone far. He was back in a moment.

"What do you say we move on to the next counter?" he asked, and they went on to look at a varied collection of bone china.

They continued on to stalls selling small furnishings, early Canadian kitchen and farm ware, vintage clothing, old beer bottles and comic books. On the weekend the place was more flea market than antique market. It was a long morning, and hard on the feet, even when they were wearing sneakers, but it passed quickly with Matt's good humor and nonsense. "Would you like something to eat or drink?" he suggested around noon hour.

"I wouldn't mind a cold drink."

"We'll see if we can find a bench and rest our weary bones."

Matt got the drinks, and they squeezed onto the end of a bench that already held two men. The bubbles of the cold drink felt good, fizzing in her mouth. She drew a weary sigh and said, "If Carr's here, he might be wearing a disguise. I think we should start checking out all people more or less his size who are wearing strange outfits, or mustaches, or beards, or hats pulled over their eyes, or sunglasses or anything that might change his looks."

"I've been doing that, more or less. And your list includes most of the men his size who are here." Matt noticed that Cathy looked tired, and said, "I'm showing you one heck of a holiday, aren't I? Let's cut out for this morning and come back this afternoon, after a gourmet lunch. It's nearly noon, and you've earned it."

It was a thoroughly tempting idea. Three hours was a long time to walk on hard pavement. "But if he comes during noon hour, we'll miss him," she said reluctantly.

"We'll catch him some other time."

She shook her head. "No, Matt. Duty before pleasure. I wouldn't goof off on a job, and I don't think you would, either, if I weren't here. I don't want to be a hindrance to you."

He gave a warmly approving smile and took her hand. "I don't think you'll be a hindrance to whatever guy is lucky enough to win you, Cathy."

She looked up, surprised at the compliment and the way he was gazing at her with admiration that bordered on love.

She felt suddenly shy. To cover it, she replied brusquely, "I bet you say that to all your helpers."

"No, only to you." His hand moved to his pocket. He was within a heartbeat of producing the English engagement ring he had bought while she was examining the old books. Before his hand moved to his pocket, Cathy emitted a gasp.

"Matt, that man!" she exclaimed, pointing to an old man dressed all in black. He wore a black hat, black suit and black shoes. A wisp of long gray hair fell below his hat. He walked with a cane and a slight limp. He was almost too good a caricature of old age to be real. "That could be Carr, dressed up."

They both rose and hurried after the man as he went into the mall. When he headed for the nearest booth selling old silver, they exchanged a meaningful look. Cathy went to his left side, Matt to his right. "Do you have any early English salt cellars?" the man inquired in a quavering voice that sounded like a parody. It was the sort of voice a younger man might adopt to impersonate an old man. And he was looking for salt cellars—small, easily portable, the sort of thing Carr favored.

Matt clamped a hand on the man's left wrist. "All right, Carr. I've got you this time!" he said triumphantly. Almost as the words left his mouth, he knew he was mistaken. The wrist under his fingers was small and frail. The flesh around the bones was loose from age. He looked at the hand and saw sparse white hairs sprouting from the blue-veined, withered hand.

"Unhand me, sir!" the man exclaimed indignantly.

Matt looked and saw a frightened old man staring at him in consternation. "I'm sorry. I'm terribly sorry. I thought you were someone else," he said.

"I'll call the police!" the man said.

"It was a misunderstanding. I hope I didn't hurt you." To cover his embarrassment, Matt said to the dealer, "Well, do you have any old English salt cellars? The gentleman is waiting."

"These youngsters today—what is to become of the world?" the old man muttered to the dealer.

Matt took Cathy's hand and they fled from the mall in shame. "I guess my idea didn't work, huh?" Cathy said. "Sorry about that."

"I'm lucky he didn't have me arrested. I feel a perfect fool."

"One of the ones who rush in. Never mind. Nobody's perfect," she consoled him. "Next time we'll follow the suspect awhile first, to check him out more thoroughly."

"Next time I'll keep my hands to myself until I see that cycle-shaped scar. I should have waited."

"No real harm is done. You gave the poor man a shock, but he'll get over it."

"I hope so."

It was second nature to keep scanning the crowd. As Matt spoke, he saw a jaunty form advancing toward the market. Hennaed hair glinted in the sunlight. Carr was wearing sunglasses, but that was his only disguise. He wasn't even wearing a hat. He had apparently been shopping, as he carried a bag with him. It was the sort of plastic bag used by supermarkets. They were being recycled by the dealers here at the antique fair. Carr had come out in full daylight. Maybe he thought the noon hour was safe. If he'd been following them, and he obviously had, he would have noticed they took their meals at regular hours. And of course he didn't know that Matt had discovered this antique market was one of Carr's haunts.

All Matt's frustration of being outwitted and humiliated came to a boil when he saw the man. He wasn't going to let Carr get away this time. He'd rush right up to him and— What if Carr pulled a gun or a knife? What if he got hold of Cathy? Matt's heart squeezed painfully at the idea. He'd have to get away from her while he went after Carr. She'd never forgive him, but at least she'd be safe, because he didn't intend to let Carr out of his sight. He racked his brain and finally came up with an idea.

"Why don't you go and get us a couple of hot dogs, while I stand guard here, Cathy? This is a good place to wait. Carr will have to come in this way if he comes at all." Carr hadn't entered the mall yet. He was looking at some of the outdoor tables.

Matt usually attended to getting their refreshment, but Cathy didn't mind going. "All right. What do you take on yours? Relish, mustard, ketchup?"

Matt had to look away from Carr to answer her. "The works," he said, and immediately looked back at Carr, but let his gaze wander a little in case Cathy suspected something. "And another soda," he added. It was sold at a different booth. It would delay her a little longer.

"I'll be right back." She hopped up and hurried toward the vending wagon.

Matt noticed that there was a good crowd around the wagon at lunchtime. Plenty of people didn't want to leave the market for lunch. He had five or ten minutes. It shouldn't take that long.

He rose just as Carr turned and moved toward the entrance to the mall. Matt was after him, dodging swiftly through the moving crowd, keeping his quarry in sight. Carr momentarily disappeared behind a group of young men, but Matt recognized his tweed jacket moving farther into the mall. That was all to the good. Better to take him in an enclosed space; it would be harder for him to break and run. Carr picked up his pace, and Matt hurried after him, accidentally bumping a few pedestrians in his flight.

Carr stopped at a counter display that had been set up in front of a shop. Matt watched as he stood, admiring the collection of sterling flatware. Carr picked up a runcible spoon and turned it over to examine the markings. After a moment he went inside the shop, still carrying the spoon.

Matt liked the idea of accosting him in the privacy of a shop. He could ask the owner to close his doors to keep things private. He picked up his pace to a run, and ran smack into the old man in black. In his haste he knocked him aside, and out of the corner of his eye, he recognized the old man. Matt had to stop a moment to help him. The man lifted the cane and hollered, "Help! Help me! This man is a lunatic!" He raised his cane to defend himself and batted the air futilely.

Matt checked to see that Carr wasn't leaving the shop, and missed the approach of a guard, who was hired because of all the valuables collected in one place. The man wore a blue shirt with a badge and a peaked cap similar to a policeman's.

"What seems to be the trouble here, sir?" he asked Matt.

Matt sized him up and figured he could take him, if necessary. "No trouble," he said, and started to run after Carr.

The old man shouted in fear and anger, and the guard took off after Matt. His strong hands reached out and grabbed the tail of Matt's windbreaker. "I'm afraid you'll have to come with me, sir."

The old man straggled forward. "That's him! That's the one! He attacked me earlier, as well. He must be a pickpocket. I'm a poor old man. I have only my pension check," he said to the guard. A tear trembled at the corner of his eye. Even Matt felt sorry for him.

Without another word the guard pulled out handcuffs and clamped them on Matt's wrists. The air turned blue with Matt's vituperation, which didn't do him anything but harm.

Inside the shop Carr studied the runcible spoon under the light, then set it aside and continued his window shopping.

Cathy found it awkward juggling two hot dogs and two cardboard cups of soda, but she didn't have far to go. Matt was right on that bench— She looked and saw two middle-aged women chatting. It must be another bench. She looked to the next one. He wasn't there, either. Looking all around, she soon concluded he wasn't anywhere nearby. He had left—and that must mean he had spotted Carr! He had gone off after Carr without telling her! The traitor!

She handed the food and drinks to a teenager loitering nearby. "Here, have some lunch on me," she said, and stalked into the mall, muttering imprecations into her collar.

The teenager looked after her, then looked at the food and took a big bite out of one of the hot dogs.

Chapter Ten

Cathy wasted the next minutes in a disjointed search of the mall. Anger clouded her reason, so that instead of making a systematic search, she just darted mindlessly from door to door. When it became obvious that she was getting nowhere, she returned to the bench where Matt was supposed to be waiting for her. It seemed strange, now, that he had asked her to get the hot dogs. Had he done it deliberately to get rid of her for a moment?

The only reason he'd do that was if he had spotted Carr. And while she waited in line for hot dogs, Matt had gone chasing Carr without her. She could forgive Matt's seizing an unforeseen opportunity, but he had planned it all to be rid of her! She was angry enough to chew nails. How could he *do* this to her? She was his partner. It was as good as a slap in the face. She was no help to him, in other words. She was nothing but a bloody nuisance. Well, to hell with Matt Wilson.

The bench, miraculously, was free, so she sat down to consider her next move. She sat with her arms folded against her chest, scowling at her lap. Abandoning the search occurred to her, only to be rejected. An Auden didn't give up that easily. She was too determined. All right, she was stubborn! There was no point trying to guess where Carr had gone with Matt in pursuit. They might have taken off on foot, or in taxis or in a boat, for all she knew. There were boats anchored not far away. Matt's desertion seemed doubly insulting, since it was her idea to come to the antique market in the first place.

After her anger simmered down, she began to have some fears for Matt's safety. Carr might be armed. Maybe he had Matt cornered.... Her heart began thumping painfully against her ribs, and her breaths came short and fast. No, don't even think it. Be calm, rational. You're a cop. Start acting like one. What should she do? No point calling the local police. They wouldn't know where to begin looking, either. There was nothing she could do but wait. Matt would come back here as soon as possible. He'd abandoned her here. He was gentleman enough that he'd at least return for her—if he knew what was good for him.

She could return to the hotel.... She settled for phoning it instead. There was no answer in her room. The house detective had nothing to report. Maybe she should go back into the mall and have a closer look. At least it gave her something to do. Sitting still was driving her crazy. She made a more methodical search this time, checking out every store. No Matt, and no Carr. Tired, worried and becoming hungry, she suddenly found herself back at the old jewelry store where she'd looked at that ring for her mother. She stopped there a moment to rest, thinking of her parents. She wanted some slightly extravagant present as a way of saying thanks for all those years of nurturing and congratulations on twenty-five years of marriage.

The twenty-fifth anniversary was silver. She'd take a look in one of the old silver shops, since she was just killing time, anyway. There was one across the aisle. She worked her way over and stood, looking at the window display—everything from ornate Victorian flatware to goblets and tea sets and some bizarre items obviously designed for an elegant table, but just what function they served she couldn't imagine.

In the shop Jim Carr peered up from his browsing and gave a start of alarm as he recognized the woman at the window. He stepped hastily behind a pillar. When he emerged a moment later, he was wearing a straw hat not unlike Cathy's. A pair of horn-rimmed glasses concealed his eyes, and a brown mustache drooped to hide the shape of his lips. He saw at once that the woman had entered the shop and was speaking to the clerk.

He strolled nonchalantly toward her, listening and watching. She was asking the clerk about a tray. Carr picked up a silver frame in his left hand and turned it over as if checking its markings. The woman still didn't pay any attention to him. He edged closer. While his left hand made a distracting flourish with the frame, his right hand reached for the flap of her purse. . . .

"That's quite all right," Matt said, rubbing his wrists to regain circulation when the cuffs were off.

"We have to look into complaints. You understand," the security guard explained.

"I am sorry," the old man in black said. Matt had explained who he was. He knew by then that the old man was a retired church minister, Mr. Petty. "If I had realized you were in pursuit of a criminal, I would not have detained you."

"It's my fault. I should have watched where I was going. Please excuse me. I have to dash now."

He hurried from the guard's office out into the mall. A quick look up and down showed him that Carr had disappeared, of course, but with luck he might still be browsing. Before he began looking again, however, he had to find Cathy and explain what had happened. She'd be furious with him.

He wasn't surprised to find that she wasn't still waiting at the bench. How long had it been? He glanced at his watch. Only twenty-five minutes. Lord, it seemed like hours. The guard wasn't convinced by his ID. He had insisted on phoning John Reilly and Hunter for corroboration. It was really old Mr. Petty who had hurried things along at the end, then delayed them again with a flurry of apologies. Cathy might be around somewhere, looking for him. He'd be lucky if she was still speaking to him.

He made a quick tour of the outside tables, then headed back into the mall. He had two people to look for now: Carr and Cathy Auden. He gave a rueful smile as he passed the old jewelry counter where he'd bought the engagement ring. She'd probably throw it in his face. Maybe if he apologized very nicely and admitted that he had been a bungling, calamitous klutz without her, she'd take pity on him.

His eyes moved across the aisle to an old silver store. Not the one Carr had gone into earlier, but it was worth a look. he saw a straw hat something like Cathy's and went closer. No, it wasn't her. It was a man. He stopped and stared harder. That jacket—Carr had been wearing a heather tweed jacket, but he hadn't been wearing a straw hat. The man was the right size and shape. Better check it out. The man turned, showing his profile, and Matt saw the horn-rimmed glasses and the mustache. Didn't look much like Carr, but hats and mustaches and glasses were easily added. He was worth another look.

"Only silver-plate, of course," the clerk explained to Cathy, "but it's thickly plated and on copper. You'll notice there is no copper showing through. These trays were not used much—more of an ornament, you know."

It would be mostly an ornament for her mother, too, something fancy to hold her silver tea set that graced the center of the dining room table and had never, to Cathy's knowledge, actually been used to serve tea.

"Can I see the round one again?" she asked. She preferred the round one, but it was fifty dollars, and she had to do a quick count of her money to see if she could afford it. She hadn't intended to buy her parents' anniversary present until she went home. She reached for her purse, looking down at it to extract her wallet and surreptitiously count her money. She saw a hand silently moving back the flap. On the thumb was a cycle-shaped scar. Carr! She stood transfixed, not even daring to lift her eyes and look at his face. She felt her heart hammering in her throat and wished with all her heart that Matt was with her.

She had forgotten all about Carr, certain that Matt was off chasing him in some other part of the city. Her mind went temporarily blank. When it cleared, she thought Mace! but the can was heavy and invariably fell to the bottom of her purse. These thoughts flew through her mind in a split second and were followed equally swiftly by the determination to catch Carr, whether she had Matt's help or not.

His hand was under the long shoulder strap of her bag. If she could wrap the strap around his wrist... She made a quick, decisive movement and entwined his wrist in the leather strap. She got a firm grip on it and yanked.

"Help!" she called to the clerk. Oh, but how could she explain the long, involved story of Carr and his crime? She opted for expediency instead, and said, "This man was trying to steal my wallet. Call the police."

Only then did she lift her eyes to look at Carr. It was him, all right, behind the phony glasses and mustache and the hat. A chill like an icicle went through her heart at the murderous expression in his eyes and the grim set of his lips. He was bigger than she, stronger, and fatally determined to escape. How had he gotten here? What had he done to Matt? That Carr was free and Matt nowhere to be seen gave rise to an awful fear. She grabbed her purse and held on for dear life.

The clerk dropped the round tray, and it bounced across the floor. Never in all his years of tending the shop had anything like this happened.

Carr tried to free his wrist, which only wrapped the strap around it more tightly. He saw that his only chance was to take the whole purse, and he yanked it from Cathy's hands. At this move, the clerk was no longer in any doubt as to what was happening. The man was not only trying to steal the woman's purse, but he'd so far succeeded in wrenching it from her grasp.

He ran forward and pushed the button that would summon the guard. Carr bolted for the door, holding the purse in his right hand. Cathy grabbed a silver water jug and was after him, shouting and trying to catch him, to knock him on the head.

Matt was just advancing toward the old silver shop when he saw the man in the straw hat bolting for the door. Before long he saw a silver jug being waved above his head, and soon he recognized Cathy. Adrenaline pumped into his veins, and he whizzed forward like a bullet, wearing a fiendish smile. He hadn't performed a flying tackle since he left high school eleven years ago, but he performed one now. He leapt at Carr and caught him by the waist, bringing him to the ground. They landed in a heap, with Carr's shoulder rammed against Matt's left arm. Cathy's purse flew across the floor, leaving a trail of wallet, comb, lipstick, paper tissues and half a candy bar behind it. A sharp, knifelike pain seared through the bone of Matt's forearm.

Cathy lifted the water jug, and it landed with a resounding bong on someone's head. It was hard to tell whose head in the confusion, but the groan sounded like Matt's voice. He lifted his head and frowned just before he passed out. Fortunately he was on top of Carr.

"Matt!" Cathy ran to try to revive him. His face was paper-white with a film of perspiration on his forehead.

The clerk came pelting forward. "Congratulations! Security should be here any minute. I called them. Oh, dear!" he exclaimed when he saw the dent in the silver water jug. "You'll have to pay for that, miss."

Security arrived with commendable promptness. The guard did a double take when he saw Mr. Wilson, once again involved in some illegal escapade. Matt's eyes fluttered open, and he said in a weak voice, "Carr. Don't let him escape."

As Mr. Wilson was obviously not going anywhere, the guard hauled Carr to his feet and put the cuffs on him.

"Matt, are you all right? I'm sorry," Cathy said. She knelt down beside him and lifted his head into her lap. "I was trying to hit Carr," she explained between sniffles. Tears were sliding down her cheeks.

He opened his eyes and made a parody of a smile. "You missed."

"Call an ambulance," Cathy said to the clerk. "He's hurt."

"No, call the police," Matt managed to say through clenched teeth. The pain in his arm was so strong he felt nauseous, but through the miasma of wrenching pain, he managed to hold on to reason. This time Carr wasn't going to get away.

"Call them both," Cathy said. "Matt, I'm sorry."

"It wasn't the knock on the head. It's my arm. I think it's smashed."

"Oh, lord," she wailed.

Matt tried to get up, but the room turned black and began to wheel in giddy circles. He was vaguely aware of Cathy's arms around him, lowering him gently back to the floor as she whispered soft words of apology and consolation. Did he hear the word "love," or was he imagining it? He nuzzled his face into her lap and sighed.

Cathy gazed down at his pale face, tense with pain, and knew that for better or worse, she was hopelessly in love with Matt Wilson. She admitted what she had already known in the depth of her heart: that the only reason he'd sneaked away from her was that he was afraid something like this would happen to her. He had been trying to protect her.

She had no idea how Carr had gotten away from him or how she had come to find him. It was strange Carr stayed here once he saw Matt, but somehow it had happened. They had caught Carr. Maybe that would absolve her for hitting Matt on the head.

It took the ambulance and police seven minutes to arrive. Carr tried to talk his way out of arrest. He hadn't broken any law. "I'm an American citizen. You can't arrest me. I want to speak to the American consul."

"He tried to snatch my purse," Cathy said. "The clerk saw him."

"That's right. He pulled it right out of her hands. I saw him," the clerk agreed.

"You'll have to come down to headquarters and lay a charge, miss," the officer informed her.

"I'll be happy to. And Mr. Wilson will have some more-interesting charges to lay, as well." She noticed her scattered belongings and snatched them back into her purse.

The ambulance attendants were putting Matt onto the stretcher. He was conscious now, though in pain, and Cathy went to him. "Are you going to be all right, Matt? The police want me to go down to headquarters. I thought I'd better do it to make sure Carr doesn't get away with a warning or something. I wish I could go with you. I'll go to the hospital as soon as I can."

He put out his good hand and squeezed her fingers. Her concern couldn't be all guilt. Surely the tears meant she loved him? "I'll be all right. You're the greatest, Cathy. I think we make a pretty good team, don't you?"

She squeezed away a tear, and said, "I guess we're pretty good."

"Good? We're fantastic. Ask one of the policemen to come here, will you, honey? Carr will hire a lawyer, get out on bail and skip town if the police don't have the whole story."

"You're not in any shape to talk to them, Matt," she objected, but half her mind was relishing that "honey." Matt had never used any terms of endearment before. He didn't even seem to notice he had done it now. It was spontaneous.

"I'll just show them my ID and give them the general idea. It'll be enough to hold Carr without bail."

She called a policeman and stayed with Matt, elaborating on his information until the officer was convinced. "We'll pay you a call in the hospital after we book Carr," the officer said.

"I won't be staying in the hospital. It's only a broken arm," Matt objected.

"You look like a ghost. But if they let you out, let us know where you are. We'll have to check with the States on your story."

"Call my company head office, in Chicago. Mr. Turnbull is the general manager. He'll vouch for me and my story." Matt extracted his wallet with some difficulty, and Cathy got out his card with the number of the head office.

"This looks legit. I'll do that," the officer said, and left.

"What hospital are you taking him to?" Cathy asked the ambulance attendant.

"The Wellesley, on—"

"I know where it is," she said, smiling at the coincidence. That was where she was born and where her dad had met her mother when he broke his leg.

It was two hours later by the time Cathy had laid her charge against Carr and found her way to the Wellesley Hospital. She had spent a part of that time going over the strange coincidence of Matt's accident and her dad's. It would be ironic if Matt fell in love with his nurse. She hurried to the desk and asked for Mr. Wilson's room.

"He doesn't have a room. It was only a fracture. He can go home as soon as Dr. Weir is finished with him. If he has someone to help him, that is."

"Yes, he has someone to help him," Cathy said happily.

She waited with a small group in a green-painted hallway with many fluorescent lights that still managed to keep the place dark. It was another half hour before Matt came out, wearing a cast from above his elbow to his fingers. Four fingers poked out through the cast over his hand. He wiggled them in greeting.

"Do you realize it's the middle of the afternoon, and we haven't had lunch, yet?" he said, but his smile said more. She knew that if they had been alone, she would be in his arms. "I think we should go to the Ritz. Do they have a Ritz in Toronto?"

"No, they have a Park Plaza, and that's where you're going—to bed."

"The best offer I've had all day." He grinned. Cathy asked the receptionist to call them a cab, and they went out into the sunlight to wait.

"Does it hurt much?" she asked.

"Only when I laugh. Seriously they've given me a pain-killer. The doctor says the arm will be sore when it wears off, but it's only a fracture. No permanent damage. It'll be a nuisance wearing the cast for a few weeks."

The taxi came, and Cathy helped him in as if he were an invalid. He rather enjoyed her fussing over him. "We'll have room service bring up some sandwiches or something easy to eat, then call the police," she said.

"What happened to our hot dogs?"

"I forget. I think I gave them to a kid."

"Both of them? Why didn't you eat yours?"

"Because I was too mad at you. You spotted Carr and didn't tell me, didn't you?"

"Yes." He gave her a worried look, and said hurriedly, "This arm is beginning to hurt like the devil."

She ignored this blatant bid for sympathy. "You just sent me off to buy hot dogs to get rid of me, and I'm the one who thought of the antique market in the first place. That was dirty pool, Matt."

"The gods have already taken their revenge. Can't you be kind and forgive me? I've learned my lesson. I just didn't want you to get hurt."

"I know," she said with a satisfied little smile. "Does it hurt very much?"

"With lots of TLC, I'll recover. I think I'm going to enjoy my recuperation." He pulled her head down on his good shoulder, and she just sat there, smiling.

Chapter Eleven

The phone was ringing when they entered Matt's room, and was busy all through their late lunch. Matt's boss was the first caller. "A bonus and a raise!" Matt smiled when he replaced the receiver. "A part of that bonus is yours, partner."

Before he could say more, the phone rang again. It was the hospital, calling to confirm some information for their records. Then Matt had to phone his office again—personnel that time to arrange some paperwork regarding his hospital care. He sat with the receiver held under his ear and a sandwich in his one good hand, occasionally managing a nibble. As soon as lunch was over, he had to call the police.

Cathy felt like a fifth wheel and decided to go back to her own hotel. She brushed her hair and applied lipstick at the mirror over his dresser before leaving. When Matt hung up on his last call, she asked, "Are you going to be okay, Matt? Since you're tied up, I thought I'd run along and do a little shopping before the stores close. There are a few people I want to buy gifts for.''

He gave a guilty start. "What a selfish brute I am. I've been monopolizing your time—wasting it. But could you wait just a little longer? The police are coming around. They want a statement from you, as well. They'll be here soon." He was glad for this legitimate excuse to detain her. He didn't have Carr now threatening her life, but he was still very reluctant for her to leave him.

She agreed, but without much enthusiasm. "All right."

Two detectives came soon after that to take statements from both Matt and Cathy. "Miss Auden is in a hurry, if you wouldn't mind talking to her first," Matt said. His guilty conscience was bothering him. They asked her some questions, then said she could go. The lunch hadn't been as she had imagined it at all. She was frustrated and annoyed at having to take her leave of Matt under the eyes of the police.

"Can you manage on your own with one arm?" she asked him before leaving.

"Luckily it was my left arm. I'll be all right."

"How does it feel?"

"Sore, but the doctor gave me some more painkillers to take as needed."

"You should take one and go to bed early." They exchanged a glance that expressed their frustration at not being alone.

Matt said, "I'll call you. Thanks for everything, Cathy. I couldn't have done it without you."

He began to get up to accompany her to the door, but one of the policemen said, "Allow me," and beat him to it. Not even one minute alone.

Cathy wandered disconsolately around a few shops. She got a record for Rob, a bottle of after-shave for her father and some chocolates for her mother, then took a cab back to her hotel. She was in her room by six. By six-thirty she was bored and angry and beginning to wish she had never come to Toronto.

Unless she called on Matt, it wasn't likely she'd be seeing him again. He shouldn't go out that night, after his accident, and she'd be leaving in the morning. Even if she went to his hotel, he'd probably be sleeping. Oh, he'd call, as he'd said he would, and thank her. He was too much of a gentleman not to do that. He'd try to make her take part of his bonus, too. She had been hoping for something different. What did she think, that because they'd had a few days together, he belonged to her forever more?

What difference did it make, anyway? He lived in Chicago. He was a busy man, darting all over the world on his glamorous job. When his arm was better, his company would probably send him to Hawaii, or England, or France on another job. It was best to make a clean cut.

When—if—he phoned, she'd say she was dead tired and go to bed. Unless, of course, he needed her. She was tired, and her plane left at ten in the morning, which meant getting up at seven-thirty or eight to give herself plenty of time. The airport was at Malton, several miles north of Toronto, and the air bus left the hotel at eight-fifteen. So the adventure was over. Time to forget Matt Wilson and get on with her life. She went to the window and looked down on the ant-size life in progress below. She felt as small and insignificant as those miniatures down below. Forget him? Maybe, in about ten years.

She tried to decide what to do about dinner. She wasn't hungry yet after that quick sandwich, but she knew she wouldn't last until morning without eating something. She could have dinner sent up. It wasn't much fun eating alone in a hotel dining room. She always felt as if people were staring at her, pitying her. She could just grab a bite at the coffee shop. It wasn't much fun eating alone there, either, or in your room, for that matter.

Well, she certainly couldn't eat anything for a couple of hours, so she'd just see what was on TV. She was moving to the set when the knock came at the door. Her heart jumped. Carr! was the first thing that came into her mind. Silly—he was locked up. Matt, was the next name that occurred to her, but obviously it wasn't him. His arm was sore; he was going to take a painkiller and go to bed.

She peered through the peephole and saw a young man in the hotel uniform. He was carrying something in a big box. She opened the door, and he handed her a florist's long box. "Miss Auden?" he said.

"Yes." She remembered to give him a tip, then slowly opened the box. It was a dozen red roses. What a nice way of saying thank-you. She read the card, already knowing who it was from, but curious to see what message Matt had sent. "Love, and thanks, and hugs, and kisses. I miss you already, Matt."

I miss you already? He must have ordered these minutes after she left—right about the time she started missing him. Love? Love had so many meanings. She took the flowers into the bathroom and arranged them in the ice bucket, since the room didn't have a vase. She put them on the desk and touched them, one by one. Sending flowers was a lovely gesture, but a rather foolish one. Matt knew she was leaving in the morning. She couldn't take them on the plane with her. But she knew one would be pressed between the pages of the book he had given her.

When the second knock came, Cathy didn't think it was Carr, but she was curious to see who it was. That time, the young man was carrying a bottle of champagne in an ice bucket on a tray with two glasses. "Miss Auden?" She tipped him again and carried the tray to the desk, wondering about those two glasses. There was no card, but she

knew who had sent the wine. Were the two glasses the hotel's idea, or had Matt asked them to bring two? He knew
she was alone....

Surely he wasn't planning to get up off his sick bed and
come here! She strode to the phone and called him, planning to forbid him to come, although she was willing to be
talked into going to his hotel. No answer. Maybe the painkillers had put him to sleep. She'd let it ring. The phone was
near his bed, and a painkiller wasn't a sleeping pill. He'd
answer after a few rings. Eight rings later, she hung up. He
was obviously already in a taxi on his way to her.

She tried to be angry with him for coming, but her heart
wouldn't let her. It was bounding with joyous anticipation.
Her whole body was bubbling with joy. She grabbed her best
dress and scurried into the bathroom to get ready. When the
third knock came at the door, she knew it was Matt. It had
to be. He'd already sent flowers and champagne. What else
was there to send—or bring—except himself?

She opened the door, trying to scowl, but her eyes were
glowing and a hesitant smile settled on her lips. Who
wouldn't smile to see the man she loved with a black evening jacket hung over his shoulders like a cloak and his
broken arm held, not in a white cotton sling, but in an elegant silk paisley scarf, patterned in red and black?

"You should be in bed," she scolded.

"And here I thought I'd have trouble convincing you of
that!" he said, and stepped in, eyes dancing. He looked
around until he spotted the flowers and champagne.

"How did you get all dressed up with your arm?"

"I used the other one, and a little help from Officer
Leahy."

"Matt, you didn't have to do all this, you know."

"Since I didn't want you to have to cut my steak and feed
me in public, I thought we'd dine in tonight. We'll want the

proper ambience for—whatever develops." She read some message in the sparkle of his bottomless, dark eyes.

"What develops will probably be complications of that fracture," she scolded.

"I certainly hope so. Like me, you foresee a strenuous evening, then? Shall we begin by uncorking the wine?"

She hid her anticipation under a veneer of annoyance. "I've never uncorked champagne in my life. I'll probably spill half of it. And I don't even have a corkscrew."

"You don't need one for champagne. I can't show you how to do it, but I'll tell you. First you undo the foil and unscrew the wires over the cork. Then nudge the cork out with your two thumbs."

It was hard to uncork wine when your fingers were trembling uncontrollably. After considerable work, the cork flew out and shot across the room, ricocheting off the wall and bouncing off a lamp before falling to rest on the desk. "You missed me," Matt said.

"That cork's a lethal weapon." She poured two glasses and handed one to Matt.

"Here's to your success," she said, touching her glass to his.

"That's a bit premature," he murmured, smiling over the rim of his glass. Light from the lamp caught it, reflecting a circle of prisms.

"Premature? You've already caught Carr."

"*We've* caught him. I'm after a different subject now." His eyes rested on her face, moving slowly from hair to eyes to her lips, where they lingered as a small smile crinkled the corners of his eyes. "One doesn't pursue an ordinary thief with wine and flowers. That's reserved for a thief of hearts."

"Oh, if that's the case, I'm caught. I'll give it back. Your heart, I mean. Not the champagne."

"I don't want it back, Cathy." He took her hand and led her to the bed, where they sat, side by side, sipping champagne. "It was more an exchange I had in mind." While Cathy sat mentally expanding on that pregnant statement, he went on to more mundane matters. "Now, about dinner. Are you up to cutting two steaks, or shall we order something precut?"

She moistened her lips nervously. "There's no hurry."

"A fine dinner was the third corner of my strategy," he explained. "Flowers, wine, dinner, and—"

She shimmied a few inches away from him. "What was the fourth corner, or dare I ask?" she inquired suspiciously.

"You don't have to run! I'm wounded. I couldn't overpower you if I wanted to, which I don't. Don't intend to *try*, I mean. Not that I don't *want* to." He pinched his lips in exasperation at his own clumsiness. "I'm babbling. Forgive me."

"Then I won't be needing my Mace."

"No, and you won't have to knock me on the head with the water jug, either. A simple 'no' will do." His eyes flickered uncertainly to hers. "But a 'yes,' of course, is what I'm hoping for," he added softly.

It couldn't be the champagne that was making her light-headed. She'd only had a sip. She took another, trying for an air of nonchalance, but her convulsive swallow betrayed her agitation. "Before I give an answer, what—what was the question?" she asked.

Matt patted her hand, and said, "It doesn't do to rush into these things. Have another glass of wine."

"Are you trying to get me tipsy?" she asked accusingly.

"No, just in an accepting frame of mind." He took the bottle and filled her glass. She took another sip, and he slowly withdrew the ring from his pocket. "I bought you something at the antique fair today, Cathy. I hope you like it."

He took out the little English engagement ring; the row of small rubies twinkled in the palm of his hand. Cathy gave a start of recognition. "Oh, Matt, you shouldn't have! I hardly feel I can accept such an expensive gift. I'm sure Mom would love it, but—"

"*Mom!* It's for *you*. You said you liked it." The words exploded out of his mouth with force. Cathy's blink of surprise told him that she hadn't been expecting a proposal. He shouldn't have rushed into it. "No strings attached, of course," he added, his lips tightening in frustration. "It's just a token to show my appreciation of your help. You deserve more. You've spent days helping me and put yourself in considerable jeopardy, as well."

She felt her heart shrivel. Just a token. Of course, the bonus he'd mentioned. "It's lovely. Thank you."

She took up the ring and tried it on her little finger, where it hung loosely. She tried it on her middle finger, but couldn't get it over her knuckle. She knew it would just fit her third finger, but hesitated to wear it there. She glanced uncertainly at Matt with a shy smile trembling on her lips.

He took the ring. "Actually *this* was the finger I had in mind," he said, and put it firmly on her third finger, left hand. Their eyes met and held in a questioning gaze.

"No strings attached," she said, trying not to make it a question, but her voice rose a little at the end.

Matt bit his lip and looked at the ring. Cathy could hardly believe her eyes. Matt Wilson unsure of himself? Matt Wilson afraid? "It's lovely, Matt. Thank you," she said demurely.

He heard the suppressed gurgle in her voice, and his eyes flew to her face. "You knew all the time I was trying to get up the nerve to propose to you!"

"No, not till this minute!" She waited expectantly for the question. "After that suggestion that we both move—temporarily—to Cleveland, I had to wonder," she said to remind him.

He batted it away. "That was before I really knew you. I've regretted it a dozen, a hundred times. What must you think of me? All that's over, Cathy. That was just sewing wild oats. I want to settle down now and be a proper husband. Split-level, suburbs, compact car. Where's my cap?" He glanced around the room for it.

"Matt, I don't expect you to turn into someone else. You're you, and I want you to go on being you."

"But aren't you afraid of my dangerous job?" he asked, a little offended. "I hate to think of *you* out risking your life. Couldn't you get assigned to a desk job?"

"Sure, I'm afraid. I'll be waiting by the phone, chewing my nails when you're out on an assignment, the way Mom waits by the phone when Dad's on a dangerous case. It goes with the territory. My job isn't actually that dangerous. Maybe when I make detective... I hope all your cases aren't dangerous?"

"Not fatally dangerous. More exciting than dangerous, usually," he said musingly. "Are you quite sure you want to be a detective?"

"Quite sure. I don't want to take your exciting job away from you, and I don't want to lose mine, either. We'll just both have to be extra careful."

He set down his glass and reached for her with his good arm. "I certainly will, now that I have someone to worry about me," he murmured into her ear. His lips brushed across her cheek, looking for her lips. "Did I remember to tell you how much I love you?" he asked in a husky voice.

"No, you didn't."

"This much," he said, and gathered her against him for a long, deep kiss.

His lips were like fire, hungry and devouring, and she relished every touch. No, she wouldn't try to change him.

She tasted the excitement and danger in his kiss and knew it was an integral part of him.

Hours later the waiter came to take away the dinner cart. They had decided that Matt would return home with her to meet her parents, since his broken arm allowed him a few days' recuperation. If he couldn't get a cancellation on her plane, he felt sure his company could arrange something on another flight.

"You'll be there for my parents' twenty-fifth anniversary party," Cathy said.

"We'll get the film developed and make up that album for the occasion."

"And a picture of us to show that the saga continues," she added.

"We should have our picture taken in front of that church where your parents were married," he suggested, getting into the spirit of it. "That's where I first saw you. I'd like it for my own album. Will your parents be shocked that we're engaged when we've only known each other a few days?"

"I don't see why they should be. They got engaged shortly after they met."

"It must be these casts that make us irresistible," Matt said, smiling contentedly at his cast. "You start by taking pity on us, and everyone knows that pity turns to love."

"And what happens when the cast comes off?" she asked. "My parents have been happily married forever, practically."

"By then, you've learned how lovable we are. You realize you can't live without us. Or do I mean we can't live without you?" he added, his smile softening to love. "All it takes is the cast to get the ball rolling."

"It took more than that, really, didn't it?" she asked, thinking over the past days. "It took a crook, and a camera, and several break-ins, and several fruitless chases."

"And two people who would have fallen in love without any of that," he added. "We were lucky that we were both here, in this town, at the same time, on the same street. Fate."

"Yeah, a lucky break," she said. "It runs in my family."

* * * * *